"I need your opinion on a very serious matter."

"What is it?" Sabrina asked her housemate, Morgan.

"I just went shopping, and I'm having second thoughts. What do you think of my new top?" Morgan spun around in a slow circle, showing off a sparkly turquoise tank top.

"I love it!" said Sabrina. "That's a nice color on you. And it looks great with that necklace."

"Thanks." Morgan ran her hands along her thighs. "And what do you think of my new leather pants?"

Sabrina nodded. "Those are great. They fit perfectly, like they were custom made!"

"And what about my shoes?"

Sabrina looked down at Morgan's new shoes. They were hideous little heels—clear plastic, with a patch of blue faux-fur across the toes. She wanted to be subtle about it, but for some reason she just blurted out, "Blech! I hate them. They're a total eyesore!"

"Oh. My. Gosh," said Morgan, uttering each word as if it were an entire sentence. "What is your problem?"

"I don't know," said Sabrina. "I can't help myself. They're awful. Worse than that ugly backpack you bought last month that I pretended to like because you were so excited about it and I didn't want to hurt your feelings." Covering her mouth, Sabrina ran into her bedroom and slammed the door behind her. "This is bad," she said to herself.

Sabrina, the Teenage Witch® books

#1 Sabrina, the Teenage Witch
#2 Showdown at the Mall
#3 Good Switch, Bad Switch
#4 Halloween Havoc
#5 Santa's Little Helper
#6 Ben There, Done That
#7 All You Need Is a Love Spell
#8 Salem on Trial
#9 A Dog's Life
#10 Lotsa Luck
#11 Prisoner of Cabin 13
#12 All That Glitters
#13 Go Fetch!
#14 Spying Eyes
#15 Harvest Moon
#16 Now You See Her, Now You Don't
#17 Eight Spells a Week *(Super Edition)*
#18 I'll Zap Manhattan
#19 Shamrock Shenanigans
#20 Age of Aquariums
#21 Prom Time
#22 Witchopoly
#23 Bridal Bedlam
#24 Scarabian Nights
#25 While the Cat's Away
#26 Fortune Cookie Fox
#27 Haunts in the House
#28 Up, Up, and Away
#29 Millennium Madness *(Super Edition)*
#30 Switcheroo
#31 Mummy Dearest
#32 Reality Check
#33 Knock on Wood
#34 It's a Miserable Life!
#35 Pirate Pandemonium
#36 Wake-Up Call
#37 Witch Way Did She Go?
#38 Milady's Dragon
#39 From the Horse's Mouth
#40 Dream Boat
#41 Tiger Tale
#42 The Witch That Launched a Thousand Ships
#43 Know-It-All
#44 Topsy-Turvy
#45 Hounded by Baskervilles
#46 Off to See the Wizard
#47 Where in the World Is Sabrina Spellman?
#48 Witch Glitch
#49 The Truth Hurts
Sabrina Goes to Rome
Sabrina Down Under
Sabrina's Guide to the Universe

Available from Simon & Schuster

The Truth Hurts

Leslie Goldman

Based upon the characters in Archie Comics

And based upon the television series
Sabrina, The Teenage Witch
Created for television by Nell Scovell
Developed for television by Jonathan Schmock

Simon Pulse
New York London Toronto Sydney Singapore

First Simon Pulse edition June 2003

SIMON PULSE
An imprint of Simon & Schuster Children's Publishing Division
1230 Avenue of the Americas
New York, NY 10020

Printed in the United States of America
10 9 8 7 6 5 4 3 2 1

Library of Congress Control Number 2002107313
ISBN 0-689-85579-6

For Ree Goldman

Chapter 1

"Salem Saberhagen!" Hilda Spellman yelled on Wednesday afternoon. "Get in here, now!"

"You called?" asked Salem, scurrying into the living room. It was almost dinnertime and, as usual, Salem was starving. It'd been half an hour since his last snack and fifteen minutes since he'd found a stale Chee•toh in the couch cushions, and his stomach was growling.

Salem stopped short when he realized that Hilda didn't sound exactly happy. Backing up out of sight, he observed her from around the corner. Hilda was usually cheerful, but at that moment her face was a deep shade of red, which made her blond hair look almost white. Her jaw was clenched in anger, and her whole body trembled. Steam came out of her ears in short plumes. And she was angrily waving the local Boston paper in the air.

Perhaps this isn't the best time, thought Salem, pausing and considering his possible approach. As he saw it, he had two options. He could act innocent, but she'd see right through that. Or he could blame someone else, but who? Sabrina? No, Hilda wouldn't believe that her sweet and innocent niece would be capable of something devious like this. He could blame Zelda, but she'd never take the rap for him.

"I know you can hear me!" Hilda yelled. "Get in here before I bring you here myself."

"Innocent it is," Salem said, waltzing into the room and rubbing up against Hilda's leg. "What is it, dear Hilda?" he asked, with all the fake-sweetness he could muster.

Hilda's normally chipper voice was raised to a pitch of near-hysteria. "What's the problem?" she asked, too mortified at that moment to answer her feline foe. "What's the problem?"

"That *is* the question," said Salem. "Is this going to take long? I could really use some dinner."

With eyes like poisonous darts, Hilda glared at Salem. "I read the personals section."

"Ah," said Salem. "No need to thank me."

"Thank *you*?" asked Hilda.

Salem stretched and yawned. "But if you want to zap me up some filet mignon tonight, well, I wouldn't exactly complain."

"You are an animal!" said Hilda.

"Yes, that's obvious," Salem said in a tired voice.

"You know that's not what I mean," said Hilda. "This is outrageous, horrible, cruel, and, what's worse—totally typical!"

"That's what I get for trying to help!" yelled Salem. "Where's your gratitude? I think I deserve a thank-you. A thank-you and a very large bowl of caviar—you can skip the toasts. I'm trying to cut back on my carbohydrates."

"I'm too upset to have this conversation," said Hilda as she began to walk away.

"Too upset to have what conversation?" asked Zelda as she walked into the living room and placed her briefcase on the coffee table in front of the couch. Zelda worked long hours as an associate professor at Adams College and was always tired at the end of the day, but this evening she seemed particularly weary. Taking off her high heels and rubbing her feet, she said, "I've had the worst day! Three students came in today during my office hours to complain about their midterm grades. And Dr. Strenton just got a huge grant from NASA and everyone is raving about him. They've already forgotten about my highly successful paper published in *Modern Physics Cracked Open.*"

"You mean," said Hilda, reading from the paper, "you're not feeling like a spunky Ph.D. with a beautiful bod and strangely skinny legs, looking for a single male for boring conversations about astrophysics?"

"What are you talking about?" asked Zelda, with an alarmed expression on her face.

"Look for yourself!" Hilda thrust the newspaper at Zelda. "Salem took out personal ads for us. He even sent in our pictures!"

Zelda took the paper and read out loud the caption that was printed under Hilda's photo. "'Healthy blonde successful pusher of caffeine seeks man who knows how to tie his own shoes. High school degree a plus.'"

Salem tried to take this opportunity to sneak out of the room, but Zelda pointed over her shoulder and Salem suddenly found himself in four little leg cuffs, which were chained to a giant lead ball. He jerked his body, but the ball made it impossible for him to move even an inch.

"You're not going anywhere," Zelda said. "Not until you explain yourself."

"This should be good," Hilda said.

"You two are always complaining about being stuck home on Saturday nights!" said Salem. "It's time to get back out there, live a little. I was only trying to help. You're both over six hundred years old! What are you waiting for?"

"Contrary to popular belief," said Zelda with raised eyebrows, "I'm very happy with my status as a single professional. And I've been enjoying my weekly bridge game, my biweekly Scrabble match, and my monthly Other Realm book club."

"Sure you are," said Salem sarcastically. "That's why you were crying into your popcorn last weekend while watching *My Best Friend's Wedding*!"

"But you make us sound desperate in that column," Hilda said.

"I wrote the truth," said Salem. "Interpret it however you want."

"Interpret this," said Hilda. Pointing, she zapped Salem into the city garbage dump.

Once the cat was gone, Hilda clapped her hands together. "Well, Zelda, that took care of him."

"Until next time," said Zelda, squinting down at

her picture. "I can't believe he used my Ph.D. induction ceremony photo. My hair looks horrible in that."

"Do you think anyone will call?" asked Hilda.

Zelda put the newspaper on the coffee table and smiled at her sister. "I hope so. One more night alone with a romantic comedy and I don't know what I'll do!"

Salem landed with a thud on top of an old tire. Looking around, he said, "Hey, I think I smell a pork chop!"

After combing through the trash for a while, finding some dinner, and chasing a couple of sewer rats, Salem grew bored. He knew it was a bad idea to go back to the Spellman home. Better to let Hilda and Zelda work out their anger first. Walking down the street, Salem realized he was near Adams College, where a third, less angry, Spellman lived.

Whenever someone slams a door in your face, it just means you've got to find an open window, thought Salem as he hurried to Sabrina's off-campus house. And luckily, the witch had left her bedroom window open as usual.

Salem jumped up onto the windowsill and into her lap. "Hey there, toots!" he shouted. "How's about a little company!"

"Salem!" yelled Sabrina, surprised by the sudden visitor.

"What's with you?" asked Salem.

"Better question," said Sabrina, dumping Salem off her lap and onto the floor, "why do you smell like a walking garbage dump?"

"Ever since you started college, you've been so perceptive," said Salem as he cleaned his coat by rubbing against Sabrina's dust ruffle.

"Salem, did you want something? I'm swamped with work and I'm already behind on studying for midterms," said Sabrina, sighing and turning the page of her gigantic history book.

"And I'm supposed to sympathize with you because . . . ?" asked Salem.

"Come on, I'm serious." Sabrina stood up and capped her Hi-Liter.

Salem jumped onto her desk, wrinkling her history notes in the process. "We don't have to talk. We can just sit here silently while you rub my belly."

Sabrina rolled her eyes. "You know," she said, "my aunts just called me and told me what you did to them."

"You mean how I helped them out by increasing their odds of finding men?"

"Funny, that's not quite how they put it," said Sabrina.

"Denial is the longest river in the world," Salem replied.

"I think you mean 'the Nile.'"

"Whatever. You get the point."

"Salem, you made them sound totally desperate," Sabrina cried.

"I call 'em like I see 'em! Excuse me for being honest!"

Sabrina glared at Salem.

"What? I'm not the only bad guy here. Hilda sent me to the garbage dump!" Salem said as he curled up on Sabrina's desk.

"You love the garbage dump," Sabrina reminded him.

"Yeah, but she did it to get rid of me—and without even serving me a proper dinner. I have feelings too, you know."

Sabrina sighed and shook her head. "Salem, it was a really cold thing to do. You know my aunts are sensitive and—" Sabrina stopped when she noticed Salem had started to doze off. "Hey, wake up!"

Salem opened one eye. "Spare me the lecture, Sabrina. I'm not in the mood."

Sabrina normally had more patience with Salem, but his tone that night, coupled with the fact that she was extremely stressed out with schoolwork, triggered something in her. "You are the most selfish, self-absorbed, manipulative, and nasty cat I've ever met!" said Sabrina, just as Roxie King was opening the door to their bedroom. Her dark-haired, cynical but kind housemate had a soft spot for Salem, so she was particularly horrified to find Sabrina yelling at him. Of course, as far as Roxie knew, Salem was just a cute and cuddly cat.

"Sabrina, what are you doing?" asked Roxie, rushing into the room.

Sabrina glared at Salem, who grinned at her mockingly. "Um, I, uh, I, nothing."

"You were yelling at Salem!" Roxie walked over to Salem, scooped him up, and began petting him. "There, there, Salem. Don't let Sabrina bother you. She's just acting mean because she's stressed out with work, but she shouldn't take it out on poor little you."

Salem purred loudly.

Roxie kissed the cat on the top of his head and then scrunched up her nose. "Wow, that is one bad-smelling cat!"

"Geh!" said Salem under his breath as Roxie set him down gently on the floor.

Sabrina rolled her eyes. "Careful, I think he's been trolling the garbage dump. But seriously, I wasn't yelling at him."

"No?" Roxie shot Sabrina a skeptical glance. "Then what were you doing?"

Sabrina panicked and blurted out the first thing that came to her mind. "I was, uh, rehearsing."

"Rehearsing?" Roxie said, raising one eyebrow in disbelief.

"Yes." Sabrina nervously tucked a strand of hair behind her ear. "The Drama Club is putting on this new play."

"Wow, and you're trying out for it? I'm really surprised," said Roxie.

"How come?"

"Well, you're always complaining that you're so busy. You know—with your classes, your job at Hilda's Coffeehouse, and the newspaper internship, you always say that you don't have time for a social life. I mean, didn't you even skip a party last weekend to write that English paper? I never thought you'd have time for a school play."

"Well." Sabrina gulped. Roxie had her there. Still,

she had to come up with an answer. "I think it's good to be well-rounded. And, um, extracurricular activities are an important part of college life."

"So what's the name of the play?"

Glaring at Salem, Sabrina said, "It's called, *The Enemy Is My Cat.*"

Roxie tilted her head to one side. "I've never heard of that. What's it about?"

Sabrina smiled. "I don't really know yet. I'm just a few scenes into it."

"Who wrote it?"

Sabrina coughed, wishing her housemate would let up with the questions. "A very obscure playwright. You've probably never heard of him."

"Try me," said Roxie. "I was pretty into theater in high school."

"You acted in school plays?" Sabrina asked, surprised because Roxie wasn't exactly what most people would call a joiner. She didn't like clubs or organizations, sororities or sports teams, study groups or societies. She had a very successful independent radio show on campus called *Chick Chat,* and that was the only extracurricular activity she participated in—probably because she was able to rant and rave on air about everything that irritated her and, for Roxie, that covered a lot of territory.

"Don't look so surprised, Sabrina," said Roxie. "I didn't act in plays. Please, actors are so self-absorbed, so conceited, and so vain."

Suddenly Morgan Cavanaugh poked her head into the room. "Are you guys talking about me?" she asked brightly.

Morgan wasn't insulted. Their redheaded resident adviser seemed unfazed by how her housemates and the world in general viewed her. Shoes, clothes, makeup, and hair: These things mattered to Morgan. She was self-absorbed, conceited, and vain—and proud of it.

"No, we weren't talking about you," said Roxie.

"Oh," said Morgan, leaning against the door frame. "Then what's up?"

"I was about to tell Sabrina that I was into theater tech in high school," said Roxie.

"Huh?" Morgan and Sabrina said at the same time.

Roxie explained, "I did a lot of the behind-the-scenes work—set design, stage construction, lighting, and sound. You know, all the stuff that no one thinks about."

"All the stuff for losers," said Morgan, crossing

her arms over her chest and looking at Roxie with pity.

Roxie responded by throwing a pillow at Morgan.

Morgan ducked out of the way, saying, "I was only trying to help you out. You know, college can be a time for transformation, for shedding your past and starting afresh."

"Morgan, I had no idea you were so spiritual," said Sabrina.

"Yeah," said Morgan. "Anyway, you agree with me, right? Will you try to convince Roxie that it's not too late to do something about her hair? I mean, hello! Haven't you ever heard of highlights?"

"Ugh!" said Roxie, sinking down onto her bed, surprised at how shallow her housemate could be.

"So why the theater talk?" asked Morgan, much to Sabrina's dismay. She wanted more than anything to change the subject. It didn't help that Salem was smirking at her from one corner of the room. It seemed so unfair, especially considering that it had been Salem's fault she'd had to lie in the first place.

"Sabrina was just telling me about a play she's rehearsing for," Roxie informed Morgan. Turning back to Sabrina, she asked, "So when are tryouts?"

"Tomorrow," said Sabrina, feeling very uncomfortable.

Morgan squealed and clapped her hands. "I love plays. What's it called?"

"*The Cat Is My Enemy,*" said Sabrina.

Roxie looked at Sabrina curiously. "I thought it was called *The Enemy Is My Cat.*"

Looking too happy and content, Salem yawned and stretched.

"Right," said Sabrina. "They're still arguing about the title. There's a lot of controversy, and a lot of disorganization in this group. If I were smart I wouldn't bother trying out."

"Uh, no way," said Morgan. "You shouldn't waste your time."

"Exactly," said Sabrina. "Wait—why are you agreeing with me?"

"Because I'm going to try out for the lead," said Morgan with a shrug.

"I don't think trying out is a good idea," said Sabrina, wanting desperately to change the direction of the conversation and wishing she could have been more honest in the first place.

"Why not?" asked Roxie. Glaring at Morgan, she

added, "I was thinking about volunteering to be a stagehand."

"Oh, that's so sad," said Morgan, her voice dripping with sympathy.

"I don't think they need stagehands," Sabrina blurted out, feeling like she was digging herself into an even deeper hole.

"Why not?" asked Roxie.

"There is no stage!" Sabrina knew her answer was feeble, but it was all she could come up with.

"What? How can anyone have a play without a stage?" asked Morgan. Flipping her hair over one shoulder, she added, "And how can anyone have a play without a stunning and beautiful lead?"

Roxie rolled her eyes. "I think Sabrina's trying to tell us she doesn't want us to participate."

"That's not it," said Sabrina meekly.

"Right," said Roxie sarcastically. "I can take a hint."

"No, it's just such a small production that I think you should both save your talents for something bigger," Sabrina tried.

"The Drama Club is staging *Romeo and Juliet* in a few months," said Morgan. "Perhaps Shakespeare would be a better fit for me."

"Me too," said Roxie.

They both headed out of the room, slamming the door behind them.

"That went well," said Salem, hopping up next to Sabrina.

"Didn't I ask you to stay off my bed?" she asked.

"I don't know," said Salem. "I'm too weak with hunger to even think straight. Please feed me."

"Salem," said Sabrina. "You should go back to my aunts' house and apologize."

"Apologize for doing them a favor?" asked Salem.

"Not funny," Sabrina said, throwing a pillow at Salem just as Roxie was entering the bedroom.

"I forgot my notebook," Roxie said. Staring from Sabrina to Salem, she threw her arms up in disbelief. "Now you're throwing things at the cat? Poor, poor little Salem."

Salem purred.

"Are you hungry? How about some tuna?" asked Roxie in a baby voice. "And some milk? I think there's some in the fridge. I think it's Sabrina's, but she won't mind if you have some! It's the least she can do after yelling at you."

"Enough," said Sabrina, picking up her history

book once more, trying to show Roxie and Salem that she did in fact need to study.

"You know," said Roxie, "I think you should go out for this play. I think it would be a healthy way for you to diffuse all of this anger you have. Healthier than yelling at a cat, that is."

Chapter 2

☆

"Ugh!" Sabrina moaned as she woke up to the harsh ring of her alarm clock early on Thursday morning. She had a crick in her neck after falling asleep bent over her history book. *I hope I at least learned something through osmosis,* she thought as she glanced at the clock on her bedside table. She had only forty-five minutes until her next class so, ignoring her pain, Sabrina got out of bed and ran for the shower. Luckily she made it there before Morgan, who was infamous for spending hours in the bathroom, did.

Twenty minutes later, Sabrina was dressed in her favorite faded jeans, and a red V-neck tank top with a matching sweater, and standing in front of the virtually empty refrigerator. "Okay, Sabrina. What do you want for breakfast, cereal or cereal?" she asked herself, moving on to the sparsely stocked food pantry. "Hmm. I think I'll have . . . some cereal." Sabrina got the only clean bowl out of the cabinet and, since there was no clean silverware left, washed a spoon.

Pouring slightly stale bran flakes out of the box, she was suddenly nostalgic for high school. It wasn't that she didn't enjoy her new life—the independence, the stimulating classes, making new friends, and being exposed to a whole new world. It was just that when she was still in high school she could point up a plate of waffles, a perfectly cooked omelette, or a three-minute egg in less than a second.

Now that Sabrina lived among mortals, she had to use her magic sparingly. She didn't want any of her three housemates to know she was anything more than an average, if not a bit overly perky, college student.

So far, it had worked. Even Miles Goodman, who was obsessed with the paranormal, didn't know he was sharing a house with a witch.

Sabrina poured the last few drops of milk from the carton into her bowl and started on her breakfast. Frowning momentarily because the cereal was too bland, she swallowed, remembering that it was her choice to go to college in the Mortal Realm. Living like a mortal was a small price to pay for this luxury.

"Is that my lactose-free milk?"

"Huh?" Sabrina said. Looking up, she saw that Miles was standing over her. His thick brown hair was unruly, as usual. He was also in one of his typical outfits: baggy jeans, and a blue long-sleeve shirt, the cuffs of which fell a couple of inches above his wrists because Miles had still not perfected his laundry technique. What was out of the ordinary that morning was the fact that Miles looked very unhappy, and maybe even angry with Sabrina.

"Is it?" he asked, picking up the now-empty milk carton and waving it in Sabrina's face.

"Whoops!" she said guiltily. "Miles, I'm so sorry. I didn't realize."

"Great," said Miles, throwing the container toward the open trash can but missing by a few feet. He walked over to the carton, picked it up, and threw it into the trash.

Sabrina wished she could zap up a new half-gallon of lactose-free milk for Miles, but that was impossible. He, more than anyone else, would be suspicious. "Oh, my gosh, I'm so sorry. I thought that was my milk. The container is the same color," she said sincerely.

"If I confuse our milks I'll get hives all over my body. Not to mention the myriad of stomach issues!" Miles placed his hands on his stomach as if he was already suffering.

"What's with all the racket?" asked Roxie, poking her head out the door.

"Sabrina drank all of my milk!" Miles shrieked. "I have a test in physics today, and without a nutritious lactose-free breakfast there's just no way I'm going to pass. This is only the beginning. After failing one test my confidence will be shot. And there goes my 3.8 GPA. It'll sink lower and lower until they kick me out of school. And the next thing you know, I'll be slinging pizzas. This, my friends, is just the start of a downward spiral. So, thanks a lot, Sabrina." Miles mock-saluted Sabrina and spun on his heel.

Shrugging meekly, Sabrina finished her cereal and put her dishes in the sink. "Miles, I'm so sorry, but I need to motor or I'll be late for class. I'll pick up some more milk for you on my way home, okay?"

"I have to stay in school," said Miles, searching

frantically through the empty cabinets. "I don't even know how to sling pizza!"

"It's my fault," said Roxie with a yawn as she shuffled into the kitchen in her dark gray sweats. "I fed Salem the last of Sabrina's milk last night."

"Great," said Sabrina under her breath. "Just what Salem needed: to be rewarded for acting like a total creep."

"What's that?" said Roxie. "Are you taking your anger out on that poor little cat again?"

"No," Sabrina replied, smiling as sweetly as possible. "Whatever gave you that idea?"

"Right!" Roxie rolled her eyes, clearly not believing her. "Well, break a leg today!"

"Huh?" Sabrina said.

"Break a leg," said Roxie. "Good luck with tryouts. For the play, remember?"

"What play?" asked Miles.

Sabrina coughed and changed the subject. Pointing to the corner cabinet and pointing up some oatmeal in the process, she said to Miles, "Did you check in there? Because I think I saw some oatmeal that you can make with water."

Miles opened the cabinet. "Perfect!" he said. Flipping over the back of the package, he read the ingredients. "Wow, it's amazing how much fructose they put into these things."

Sabrina groaned, wondering if she could ever win.

"So what's the play?" Miles asked again as he filled the teakettle with water and put it on the stove.

"Nothing," Sabrina said. "I mean, it's not a big deal. I'd really rather not talk about it."

"I'm sure you'll do great," said Roxie.

Sabrina forced a grin. "Of course. Thanks. But whew, I'm a little nervous about it. Plus, I'm going to be late. Gotta go." She picked up her backpack and slung it over her shoulder.

Once outside, Sabrina breathed a sigh of relief and then rushed to biology class, sliding into her seat moments before her professor began her lecture on the ethical implications of stem-cell research.

After class, Sabrina went to the student center to get some coffee and read the latest issue of the student newspaper.

Sabrina tried to shake off her bad mood, but she was finding it difficult. The whole incident with the imaginary play had really frazzled her. She hated to lie. She didn't consider herself a dishonest person but, aside from that fact, lying was complicated. One small fib about a school play to cover the fact that she was yelling at Salem had snowballed. She wished she could be honest, but living with mortals meant stretching and bending truths, telling the innocuous little lie here and spreading a tiny bit of misinformation there. Sabrina just wished she could tell the truth 24/7. It would make her life so much easier.

As Sabrina folded up the newspaper and started to put it into her backpack, she noticed an ad in the classifieds section. It was for a free poetry-writing workshop, which met Thursdays at 8:00 P.M., and the first class was tonight.

Writing was one of Sabrina's great loves. English had always been one of her favorite subjects. She was currently interning at the *Boston Citizen.* Even though most of Sabrina's internship consisted of photocopying, ordering lunch for reporters, and picking up after staff meetings, she still got an occasional assignment, and writing nonfiction came fairly easy for her.

Poetry was new and it was different. Poetry was something she loved to read, but had never really considered writing herself. Maybe it would be fun. And maybe Roxie had been right when she'd said that Sabrina needed to find another extracurricular activity to diffuse her stress.

Well, Sabrina thought, *there's only one way to find out.* She took out her cell phone and called the number listed in the paper and enrolled herself in the workshop.

That afternoon in history when Sabrina was supposed to be focusing on the negative effects of the Industrial Revolution, she was thinking about poets and poetry: Emily Dickinson, T. S. Eliot, Walt Whitman, Robert Frost, and Sylvia Plath.

She finished up a quick three-hour shift at Hilda's Coffeehouse and then raced home, wanting to change before going to the workshop.

"Hey, how was the audition?" asked Morgan, who was catching up on her soaps in the living room when Sabrina breezed through the door.

"Not great," said Sabrina. "I don't think I stand a chance."

"How come?" asked Morgan.

Sabrina thought fast. "I totally blew my lines. I couldn't even remember the second half of this speech the main character gives, on, uh . . . the superiority of dogs over cats."

Morgan picked up the remote and turned off the television. "So let's hear it," she said.

"Um," said Sabrina feebly, wondering why she'd opened her big mouth. She could have just told Morgan she'd decided not to try out! But now it was too late; she'd lied again, and she had to cover for herself. "Cats. They shed more than dogs. They climb up on counters. They don't fetch or play ball. . . . That's all I remember."

Morgan grimaced. "That sounds like a horrible play."

"*The Enemy Is My Cat,* you mean?" asked Roxie as she walked into the room.

"Yeah," said Sabrina. "The audition went really badly, and I don't want to talk about it. In fact"—Sabrina discreetly pointed to the phone, which rang a second later—"I'll get that."

Ignoring Morgan's and Roxie's strange glares, Sabrina picked up the phone. Of course, no one was on the other end. She had triggered the ring herself so she could get out of the conversation.

"Hello? Oh hi." She cupped the bottom of the phone and whispered to Morgan and Roxie, "It's the director of the play." Speaking into the phone, she nodded and frowned. "Uh-huh. Okay. Oh. Oh, that's too bad. Are you sure? There's no way? And about the stagehands? Right, there's still no stage! Well, thanks anyway."

Sabrina hung up the phone. "Just as I suspected," she said as she flopped down onto the couch next to Morgan. "I didn't get the part."

"Who did?" asked Roxie, sitting down in the overstuffed armchair.

"Some senior," said Sabrina as she shrugged.

Morgan turned back to the television, saying, "If only that senior knew how close she came to losing the part to me!"

Roxie rolled her eyes at Sabrina, who just laughed. "I'm not too upset about it. In fact, I don't think I'd have time to rehearse someone else's lines, since I'll be busy writing my own before long."

"Hello!" said Morgan. "Trying to watch TV in here. Can you two vacate?"

"Come on. Let's go into our room. I want your help with something," Sabrina said.

Once they were in their room with the door closed, Roxie asked, "So what do you need my help with? And what did you mean by writing your own lines?"

"Well," said Sabrina, "I took your advice. About the extracurricular thing, I mean. You're right. My whole life is school, work, and internship, day after day, and I need something else to, you know, diffuse my stress."

"That's great," said Roxie. "What are you going to do?"

"I'm taking a poetry-writing workshop," said Sabrina, loving how it sounded.

Roxie nodded. "Great."

"Do you want to sign up too?" asked Sabrina. "When I called to add my name to the list this morning, they said there were still a bunch of spaces free."

"When does it meet?" asked Roxie, sitting down at her desk.

"It starts tonight at eight o'clock."

Roxie shook her head. "Thanks, but writing isn't my thing. Plus, preparing for *Chick Chat* takes up enough of my time. But have fun."

"I will," said Sabrina. "And I'm sorry about the whole play thing. I don't know what came over me. It's not that I wanted to exclude you. I promise. It's just . . ." Sabrina wanted more than anything to share her secret with Roxie, but she knew she couldn't.

Roxie held up her hands. "It's cool. I need my own space sometimes too. I shouldn't have given you such a hard time about it."

Sabrina broke out in a wide grin. "You're a great friend, Roxie."

"No need to get mushy on me," said Roxie.

"Okay," said Sabrina. Walking to her closet, she opened it up and pulled out her black cocktail dress. "What do you think of this for tonight?"

"Are you going to be in a lounge act? Or are you going to a poetry class?" asked Roxie.

Sabrina held the dress up to her body and looked down. "I guess you're right. Too dressy." She put the dress away and picked out a pair of hip-hugger jeans, instead. "Better?" she asked.

"Much."

"Roxie, phone!" yelled Morgan.

"I'll take that in the living room," said Roxie as she walked out the door. "Have fun tonight!"

Sabrina changed into the jeans and put on a purple-and-black-striped shirt, and her favorite black boots. Adding a touch of pale pink lipstick perfected her outfit. She slung her book bag over her shoulder and was off.

The workshop was taking place in the back room of a coffeehouse near campus. Half of the chairs, which were placed around a cluster of small tables, were already occupied by the time Sabrina got there. Looking around, she noticed some familiar faces. She waved to a girl with shoulder-length curly brown hair and beautiful green eyes—someone she remembered meeting at an Emerson College fraternity party.

"Hi," the girl said, waving back. "Sabrina, right?"

"Yes," said Sabrina, sitting down next to her. "And your name is . . ."

"Amber."

"Amber, of course," said Sabrina. "How could I forget? So, have you taken a poetry workshop before?"

"No, this is my first one," said Amber.

"Me too," said Sabrina, relieved that she wasn't the only person new to the workshop experience.

As Sabrina unpacked her notebook, a bubbly Asian-American young woman with short, choppy magenta hair walked in. Sabrina knew her from Adams College. They'd had music theory together last term. "Hey, Maxine," Sabrina said.

Maxine smiled warmly as she sat down.

It was almost eight o'clock, and the seats were filling up. The last person to enter sat down across from Sabrina, smiled, and winked.

His name was Tony, and he was the very cute waiter from Sergio's, her favorite Italian restaurant.

A few minutes later the instructor strode into the room. He shrugged off a jeans jacket to reveal a navy blue turtleneck, which he was wearing with a pair of light brown cords. He draped his jacket over the back of a chair and sat down. When he took off his brown fedora his thick, dark, curly hair fell down past his shoulders. Shaking it out, he said, "Welcome to my workshop. I am Max Berkowski. Let's talk poetry."

While the students watched, Max dumped a battered green canvas bag onto the floor and started pulling out old books. Once they were all on the small table in front of him, he glanced around and asked, "You. What's your name?"

Sabrina looked over her shoulder. No question Max was talking to her. His blue eyes seemed to bore right into her, making her feel like she was made of glass. "Sabrina Spellman," she said, happy that she hadn't stuttered.

"Sabrina Spellman. Great name. Very lyrical. Who's your favorite poet?"

"Um, I don't really know," said Sabrina, a little taken aback. "That's a tough question."

"Life is full of them," said Max, seemingly unimpressed. Turning to Maxine, he asked her the same question.

"Walt Whitman," she answered definitively.

"What about you?" he asked, turning to a blond guy in a blue-and-red-striped rugby. "What's your name?"

"Jason Gertz," said the guy, shifting in his seat and readjusting his white baseball cap.

"Well?" asked Max.

"Bob Dylan," said Jason.

"Okay," said Max.

"Who's your favorite poet?" Amber asked their instructor.

"Myself," said Max.

"Really?" asked Sabrina, not meaning to say it out loud.

Unfazed, Max grinned at her. "Yes. When you're an artist, self-confidence is important. Believe in yourself, be your own biggest fan." Looking around at the class, he asked, "Does that sound self-centered?"

No one answered.

Grinning, Max asked, "What do you think, Sabrina?"

Way to put me on the spot, thought Sabrina, trying to remember why, exactly, the poetry workshop had seemed like a good idea. Of course she thought her instructor sounded self-centered, but she didn't want to say so. "Not at all," she lied.

"Wrong answer again!" said Max. "You're on a roll."

Sabrina slunk down into her seat, wishing she could disappear under the table.

"Poetry is a very personal art form," Max went on to explain. "You need to look inward, and believe that your own experience matters. Thus, you need to be self-centered. Got it?"

Max continued to explain: "Poetry is about expressing your emotions, conveying raw experience. At its best, it is free-flowing, and from the heart and soul of the poet. Of course, at its worst, it's clunky and pointless."

Sabrina didn't know what, exactly, she was supposed to take from all of this, so she just sat back and listened.

Max went on and on. He was clearly someone with a great passion for words—his own, especially. "We're going to be reading a lot of student poetry," he said, finally starting to wrap things up. "I'd like you all to begin immediately, in fact. Go home, don't think about it, just pick up a pen or a pencil—or go to your computer or word processor, if you must—and write. Next week, a few students will volunteer to read their work out loud, and they'll also bring copies for everyone else so they can critique it."

"We have to share our work with everyone?" asked Amber.

Max nodded. "It won't be easy at first, but it's necessary. After all, writing is about communication, and the only way to improve is to get honest feedback."

Jason shifted in his chair and asked, "But what if everyone hates my writing?"

Max stared at the ceiling and scratched his chin as he thought. "Well, everyone should be tactful. I'm not saying you should attack one another, but on the other hand, wouldn't you rather know if something isn't working?"

"I guess so," said Jason with a shrug.

"Good," said Max, "Everyone agree?"

The class nodded. "Yes," said Sabrina. "Honesty is definitely the best policy."

"Great," Max said. "Now, who wants to volunteer to go first?" He looked around the room.

Everyone else looked at the floor or the ceiling, or stared at their notebooks in front of them.

Sabrina decided to be brave. "I'll volunteer to go next week."

"Excellent!" said Max. "Thank you, Sabrina." He scribbled her name onto a small pad. "Who else? Jason?"

"Uh, sure," said Jason, turning bright red.

"I'll go too," said Tony, jotting something down in his notebook.

"Okay," said Max as he capped his pen. He abruptly packed up his things. "That'll do it. I'll see you next week."

"What were the books for?" asked Sabrina.

"Ambiance!" With that final word, Max was gone.

Amber turned to Sabrina. "Wow, he's a pretty intense guy."

"No kidding," said Sabrina as she gathered up her things. "Next week should be very interesting."

☆

Chapter 3

☆

Can you have question marks in poems? Sabrina wondered as she crossed out the last two lines of her eighteenth version of her poem. It was Saturday night, and she planned to stay in to write. Of course, it wasn't going very well.

Sabrina read over what she had so far and decided that it was all wrong. So she tore it from her notebook and crumpled it up. She threw the ball of paper toward the trash can, but it bounced off the rim and landed a foot away, right next to four other crumpled balls. Sabrina pointed toward the discarded paper—her pathetic attempts. They all rose and then dropped into the trash can, one by one.

When she'd volunteered to have her poem critiqued, she'd already had an idea in her head of what to write. When she was on her way to the workshop she'd passed by a tiny pink flower pushing up out of a crack in the sidewalk. This small bit of nature among a sea of concrete impressed her. The flower was so strong, yet at the same time so frail. It represented to her the endurance of nature in urban environments. Even though the theme came to her easily, she was struggling to find the right words. They just wouldn't come.

Sabrina chewed at the tip of her pencil as she stared at the page, frustrated that the task was so difficult. She'd had no idea that it would be so agonizing. In fact, the writing was something Sabrina had been looking forward to since she'd left the workshop—in English class on Friday morning; when she was making cappuccinos at Hilda's Coffeehouse later that afternoon; when she went over to her aunts' house for dinner that night; and even when she was watching the *Planet of the Apes* marathon with Miles until midnight.

Finally, on Saturday morning, Sabrina had sat down to write, but there had been so many distractions, so many things to do. Sabrina had cleaned her room, and then she'd done a mud mask with Morgan. She'd helped Roxie rearrange her closet, and Sabrina had even typed up her history notes.

Eventually, though, it was late afternoon and she'd had no choice but to face the blank page.

Not knowing where to begin, Sabrina had stared at her notebook until her eyes had burned. This had gotten her nowhere. Finally, she'd decided to write things down just to get words on paper. But that hadn't helped her either.

If Sabrina's assignment had been to write a newspaper article or an essay on this topic, she'd have been done by now. But a poem? A poem was a whole different story, a whole new medium. Perhaps one that Sabrina just couldn't master.

"Knock, knock," said Morgan as she opened the door to Sabrina's bedroom. "Are you almost ready?"

Sabrina glanced at her clock. It was already nine o'clock in the evening. Where had the time gone? She looked up at Morgan, who was wearing a pink leather miniskirt with a mauve tube top and huge platform heels. "No," said Sabrina, "I just got on a roll with my new poem."

"Whatever. We're supposed to be at the Sigma Delta Theta fraternity party, like, now." Morgan looked Sabrina up and down. "You're not planning on wearing that, are you?"

Sabrina put her notebook aside and stared down

at herself. She was wearing old jeans and an oversize green sweater. Her hair was in a loose bun on top of her head—not exactly a look she wanted to show off at a campus party. "I think I'm going to have to skip the party tonight, Morgan."

"Sabrina!" said Morgan, in a tone that came dangerously close to a shriek. "As your RA and friend, I must inform you that your social life is in shambles. You already stayed in Friday night. Big mistake. You don't want to become a hermit, or end up really surly and bitter like Roxie or just generally weird like Miles. I mean, come on. You're my last hope here."

"Hey," said Sabrina. "Roxie and Miles are my friends. And there's nothing wrong with staying in on a Saturday night—especially considering that I'm struggling to write this poem that—"

Sabrina didn't get to finish her sentence because Morgan cut her off. "You're staying home to write poetry! What are you turning into? Poets are the most depressed people on earth, Sabrina!"

"I'm starting to understand why," said Sabrina, looking at her trash can, which was brimming over with her rejected drafts.

"Why don't you just write a haiku and be done with it?"

"You know what haiku is?" asked Sabrina, stunned.

Morgan glanced at her watch impatiently. "I do go to class . . . occasionally. Of course there's more incentive when there's a cute teacher." She then cleared her throat and proudly recited, "Just three lines—the first line has five syllables, the second seven, and the last, five."

"I think this workshop is more about expressing emotions and ideas than memorizing the number of syllables in a line," said Sabrina, remembering what her instructor Max had said.

"Oh, come on," said Morgan. "Everything is about the numbers. And we'll be a lot of numbers late if you don't wrap this up. Here, I'll write one for you."

"A girl sits and waits
For inspiration to strike
Can you spell loser?"

"Wow, that's not bad," said Sabrina. "So is it okay to have a question mark in a poem?"

Morgan ignored her question and shot off another haiku.

"Sabrina come on
It's getting late we must go
To the party now!"

"You make it look so easy," said Sabrina. Pen poised, she tried one herself:

A single flower
Rises through the concrete
Crack. Nature endures where humans fall short.

Sabrina ripped the page out of her notebook and crumpled it, crying, "I can't even write a haiku!"

"Look, are you coming to this party or not?" asked Morgan.

"Not," said Sabrina. "Maybe next weekend. Sorry."

"And I had such high hopes for you," said Morgan as she closed Sabrina's door behind her.

"Finally some peace and quiet," said Sabrina.

As she stared at the blank page, the peace and quiet started to get to her, so she flipped on the radio.

And then she fell asleep. . . .

Sabrina rushed to her workshop the following Thursday night, feeling like she had a million butterflies swarming around in her stomach. She'd agonized over the poem for days but, in the end, it had all been worth it. On Wednesday night, after losing count of how many hours she'd spent working and with no idea of how many drafts she'd been through, it had come to her. All at once—the lines seemed to flow magically. It was like someone else was moving her pen for her—straight from the depths of her soul onto the pages of her notebook. Just like Max had described! The coolest part was, she hadn't even used magic. And even better than that, Sabrina was sure that the final product was, to put it mildly, a masterpiece.

In her excitement to share her perfect poem with the world, Sabrina arrived at the workshop twenty minutes early, with copies of her poem for her classmates, just like Max had asked for. She took a seat and opened up her book bag.

"Hey, how's it going?" asked Amber as she walked into the room.

Sabrina smiled as she pulled out her notebook and copies of her poem. "Good, how are you?"

"Not bad. You missed the best Sigma Delta Theta party last weekend!" Amber said, taking off her giant fisherman's sweater and placing it over the back of her chair.

"I know," said Sabrina proudly. "I was working on my poem."

"You skipped a Saturday night fraternity party to write?" asked Amber, her green eyes wide in surprise.

"That is a wonderful thing," said Max as he walked into the room and sat down across from Sabrina.

"Thank you," said Sabrina.

Taking off his hat and shaking out his hair with a flourish, Max said, "The year before I had my first book published, I hardly saw the light of day."

"Really?" said Sabrina.

"How many books do you have published?" asked Amber.

"Four," said Max.

"So you're, like, a famous poet?" Amber asked.

"Poets aren't famous," said Max, grinning. "Not in their own lifetime, anyway. I think you have to die a tragic death or just have a really miserable life to get noticed."

"That's heavy," said Amber.

"You stayed inside for a year?" asked Sabrina, thinking about how hard it had been to sacrifice just a few days of fun.

"At times I went weeks without seeing or speaking to another human being," said Max.

He seemed proud of this fact, but it was something that made Sabrina shudder.

As the rest of the class streamed in and took their seats, Max checked the clock. Staring at the empty chair in one corner of the table, he said, "Someone chickened out."

Sabrina looked around the room and realized that Jason, the guy who was supposed to read his poem that night, was missing.

"No matter," said Max. "Sabrina, why don't you go first?"

"Okay," said Sabrina. She handed out copies of her poem to the class. Smiling and sitting up a little straighter, she read, "It's called 'A Touch of Green.'

"More comfort than you can imagine
Like a breath of fresh air
Is this single stem
One hint of green
Amidst the vast sea of concrete
Develop demolish develop again
The flower emerges with no plans
That nature didn't write."

"Well done, Sabrina," said Max. Looking around at the class, he added, "So, don't be shy. What does everyone think?"

Even though she really loved her poem, Sabrina didn't want to seem like she was expecting praise, so she looked down at her notebook. Still, her ears burned red in hopes of positive feedback.

Some time passed, and no one had said a word. Sabrina looked up. The class just gave her blank stares.

Max broke the silence. "Tony, what did you think?"

Tony shifted in his seat. "I think it was beautiful. Great job, Sabrina."

"Me too," added Maxine. "Good use of free verse. It's nice that you weren't tied down by any specific form or structure."

"I agree," said Amber, admiring her freshly painted red nails. "I like it."

"Thanks," said Sabrina meekly, wondering why everyone looked so uncomfortable. No one had hated her poem, but no one had loved it either. That was the problem. Sabrina had spent hours writing. Sharing her poem with the class felt like sharing part of her soul. Yet not one person in the workshop had been moved enough to express a strong opinion.

She may as well have read the menu board from Hilda's Coffehouse. Frustrated, Sabrina turned her head away from everyone, covered her mouth, and quietly recited a spell.

"It's the truth I seek
So don't be meek.
With the blink of an eye
You won't be able to lie."

Sabrina waited for the spell to take effect.

"So," said Sabrina, crossing her arms over her chest and looking at Amber, "what did you really think of my poem?"

"To be honest, I wasn't listening," said Amber.

"Why not?" asked Sabrina.

"I don't know," said Amber. "I just, like, had other things on my mind. Like, I'm not sure if my nail polish matches my outfit. It looked like it did in the bottle, but once you apply it, the shade is never exact. Have you noticed that?"

This was not exactly what Sabrina was expecting!

Shrugging, she turned to Maxine. "You said before you admired the lack of structure in my poem. Is that what you really think?"

"Not really," said Maxine, running her fingers through her hot pink hair. "I was just saying that to try to impress our instructor."

"It worked," Max quipped. "I love it when my ideas are repeated back to me, verbatim."

"Oh, but I did like the poem a lot, though," Maxine added.

Sabrina sighed in relief. "I'm so glad."

Maxine went on. "You really capture the nature of a true first love—you know, something that stands against all odds."

"You thought my poem was one about true love?" asked Sabrina, amazed.

"Well, yes," said Maxine. "You mean it wasn't?"

Sabrina didn't answer her question. Instead, she turned to the rest of the class. "Please raise your hands if you thought my poem was about true love."

A few students raised their hands. Sabrina was happy that not everyone had misinterpreted her work.

"What about you, Max? What do you think of my poem?" Sabrina asked.

"Oh, I don't know," Max said with a yawn. "I wasn't really paying attention when you read it. I was thinking about this scene for my latest screenplay."

Turning to another student—a cute, shy guy in the corner—Sabrina asked, "What were you thinking about while I was reading my poem?"

"I was wondering if you were a natural blonde," he said.

Deciding that she'd endured enough honesty for the day, Sabrina sat down as the class talked among themselves. This was definitely not what she had hoped for when she had so carefully crafted her poem. Sabrina quietly un-cast the spell, since she no longer needed it.

"So now you've heard it word for word
The whole-truth thing can be kind of absurd.
But don't you worry, fret, or frown
If you're feeling kind of down.
With the point of one finger
The Honesty Spell will no longer linger."

A moment later, Max's comment told her the reversal had worked.

"As I was saying," said Max, "I can really tell you wrote from the soul, and that's a beautiful thing."

"Thanks," said Sabrina, smiling.

"Who's next?" asked Max. "Who else will share a poem tonight?"

"I will," said Tony, standing up and clearing his throat. "Slinging pizzas, to and fro, making pasta from fresh new dough . . ."

Sabrina didn't hear Tony's poem. She tuned him and the rest of the workshop out, because she had too much on her mind. While it's true that Sabrina had hoped the others would really like her poem, that wasn't the only thing that was bothering her. She genuinely wanted some constructive criticism.

When the workshop ended, Sabrina was still a bit down, but by the time she made it home she felt better. She'd learned something from the experience, after all: Perhaps brutal honesty isn't always the best policy.

"Oh good," said Morgan as she made her way downstairs—carefully, because she was trying to balance on a pair of spiked heels. "I'm glad you're back. I need your opinion on a very serious matter."

"Great," said Sabrina. "What is it?"

"I just went shopping, and I'm having second thoughts. What do you think of my new top?" Morgan spun around in a slow circle, showing off a sparkly turquoise tank top.

"I love it!" said Sabrina. "That's a nice color on you. And it looks great with that necklace."

"Thanks. They're black pearls," said Morgan,

touching her necklace with her fingertips. "A gift from Daddy before he stopped caring." Morgan's credit card bills were so high that her father had cut her off months ago, but she still seemed to feel the sting of it afresh every day.

"Cool," said Sabrina.

Morgan ran her hands along her thighs. "And what do you think of my new leather pants?"

Sabrina nodded. "Those are great. They fit perfectly, like they were custom made!"

"Don't I wish," said Morgan. "And what about my shoes?"

Sabrina looked down at Morgan's new shoes. They were hideous little heels—clear plastic, with a patch of blue faux-fur across the toes. She wanted to be subtle about it, but for some reason she just blurted out, "Blech! I hate them. They're a total eyesore!"

"What?" said Morgan, placing her hands on her hips, clearly outraged.

Sabrina was surprised that she'd been so blunt. "I didn't mean it," she said. "I'm sorry, Morgan. It's just that . . ." Sabrina tried to think of a compliment to appease Morgan. After all, it wasn't a life-or-death situation—it was only fashion, and Morgan had already made the purchases, so what did it matter? But her mind was blank. All she could think about was the fact that Morgan's feet looked huge in the shoes, and even though Sabrina didn't want to, she told her so. "You look like Bigfoot in those!"

"Oh. My. Gosh," said Morgan, uttering each word as if it were an entire sentence. "What is your problem?"

"I don't know," said Sabrina. "I can't help myself. They're awful. Worse than that ugly backpack you bought last month that I pretended to like because you were so excited about it and I didn't want to hurt your feelings." Covering her mouth, Sabrina ran into her bedroom and slammed the door behind her. "This is bad," she said to herself. "This is very bad."

Morgan was pounding on the door, so Sabrina pointed and locked it. Then she booted up her computer. Something had gone very wrong with the Honesty Spell, and she had to figure out what it was.

Chapter 4

☆

"The fine print!" Sabrina cried as she read the dreaded words on the Witch Wide Web. "Why is there always fine print?"

Sabrina cursed herself for being so careless. Then she clicked on the fine print and enlarged it. As she read, her heart sank, as if it had up and left her body and had wandered into a pile of quicksand.

"Do not, under any circumstances, cast and uncast an honesty spell within an hour-long period. If this happens, the witch responsible will be forced to speak honestly for forty-eight hours. No ifs, ands, buts, or exceptions," it said. *Whoops,* thought Sabrina. It was her biggest understatement of the day.

Morgan started pounding at her door, yelling, "What's the deal, Sabrina?"

"I was just being honest," said Sabrina—honestly.

"I didn't mean to hurt your feelings."

"That's the last time I ask for your opinion," said Morgan.

"Can't talk right now." Sabrina typed at the computer keys furiously, searching the WWW's database. While every spell had fine print, every spell also had a loophole.

"Aha!" said Sabrina as she located the section she was looking for. She propped her elbow up on her desk and leaned in to read. "There are two ways that a witch under an honesty spell can avoid speaking the truth. First, by clamping a hand over her mouth, and second, by diverting the truth."

Huh? thought Sabrina as she clicked on some more keys until she could find a better explanation. "To divert the truth one can speak another, unrelated truth."

Sabrina reached for the power switch and turned the computer off. She calculated that she had cast and then un-cast the spell at around 8:20. Until that time, Saturday, she'd have to stay on her toes. Either speak the truth or, whenever possible, avoid all human contact. Was it possible? She hoped so. She didn't have any other options.

Sabrina decided to try out her newfound loopholes. Going into the common area, she found

Morgan eating sushi at the dining room table.

"Don't even say it," said Morgan, pointing her chopsticks at Sabrina and looking away.

"Ask me again," said Sabrina, noticing that Morgan had changed out of her ugly shoes and into a pair of silver platform sandals.

"Ask you what?" asked Morgan.

Sabrina shrugged. "I don't care. Ask me anything."

"Why are you acting like such a witch?" asked Morgan.

Okay! That was a tough one. "Because I—" Sabrina covered up her mouth with her hands and it worked—she was about to tell Morgan that she was, in fact, a half-witch, and that if she really wanted to call anyone a witch, then she should do so to Hilda and Zelda, but she caught herself before the truth escaped from her lips.

Morgan popped a spicy tuna roll into her mouth and observed Sabrina as if she were some kind of freaky specimen in biology lab.

"Ask me something else," said Sabrina.

Washing her food down with a sip of Diet Coke, Morgan asked, "Why did you say those horrible things about my shoes?"

Sabrina employed tactic two of the loophole diversion, saying, "I really like your hair."

"Huh?" said Morgan, wondering what that had to do with anything.

"It's such a pretty shade of red," said Sabrina. "And it's so natural, too. I've always admired it."

"Thanks," said Morgan, smoothing out her bangs and forgetting all about her original question.

Sabrina smiled, happy that the loophole was working so well.

Just then Miles walked into the room. "Hi, Sabrina."

"Hi, Miles. How's it going?" she asked.

"Good. How are you doing?"

"Oh, horrible," said Sabrina. "I had the worst night at my poetry workshop. You see, I cast—" Sabrina covered her hand with her mouth.

"What were you saying?" asked Miles, glaring at Sabrina like she'd just sprouted a second head.

Not wanting to spill the beans, Sabrina spoke the first truth that came to her mind. Unfortunately for Miles, it turned out to be kind of a rude one. "Those jeans are too big on you."

"Huh?" said Miles, looking down at his jeans.

"She's right, you know," said Morgan, picking up

the ball and rolling with it. "You are a fashion basket case. Everything you own is either too baggy or too tight."

"I came out here to see how Sabrina's workshop went and this is the thanks I get?" asked Miles. "What's the deal?"

Sabrina thought hard, trying to come up with something nice to say to Miles. "I'm going to buy you more lactose-free milk tomorrow."

Miles turned to her. "Thank you. And that has to do with . . ."

Sabrina covered her mouth, ran into her room, and slammed the door behind her.

"Whew!" she said as she slumped down with her back against the door. "That was a close one."

"What was a close one?" asked Salem, who was perched atop Sabrina's desk, rereading her copy of Machiavelli's *The Prince,* his favorite book, which is about seizing and maintaining power.

Sabrina covered her mouth until the urge to tell Salem the truth passed.

"Fine, don't tell me," said Salem. "If you'll notice, I haven't been coming around here lately."

Sabrina sank down onto her bed. "I really need to be alone right now."

"Okay," said Salem. "I can take a hint. And I guess we'll be seeing plenty of each other soon enough, but you don't have to be so . . . honest!"

"Oh, but I do," said Sabrina. Pointing, she zapped Salem back to her aunts' house.

Deciding that a better plan was to avoid all contact with humans, Sabrina changed into her pajamas and got into bed with her giant history book. A few minutes later she was interrupted.

"Hey Sabrina, how was the workshop?" asked Roxie.

Sabrina wished she could tell her roommate that she was tired and didn't want to talk about it. But that would be a lie; Sabrina was too wired to sleep. Her mind reeled as she tried to come up with something true but innocuous to say. "The workshop was—perfectly warm."

"Huh?" said Roxie.

"The temperature at the back of the coffeehouse."

"Yeah?" said Roxie.

"Well, the first week it was a little cold. But tonight it was just right."

"Fascinating," Roxie said sarcastically.

"I know that's not a very interesting detail," said Sabrina, trying to bury her face in her book.

"So what else?"

"Um," said Sabrina. "One of the guys—his name is Jason—he was supposed to read a poem today and he didn't show."

"But you read your poem?" asked Roxie.

"Yes," said Sabrina, faking a yawn.

"Are you tired?" asked Roxie.

"No," said Sabrina.

"Then why the yawn?"

Sabrina covered her mouth with her hands to keep from saying, "I was faking a yawn so you'd stop asking me all of these questions."

Roxie gave Sabrina a sideways glance. "Why are you acting so strange?"

Sabrina nodded. "I'm trying out a diversion technique. Whoops! I didn't mean to say that." Sabrina covered her mouth with both hands.

"A diversion technique," said Roxie. "Oh wait, I get it. Is it because the poetry workshop went badly?"

"You could say that," Sabrina mumbled, weakly.

"Okay, if you don't want to talk, I'm not going to force the issue."

Sabrina beamed. "That's exactly it. I don't want to talk about it!"

"I'm sorry. I know how hard you worked on that poem. Geez, people really stink, huh?" Noticing that Sabrina was reading a textbook, Roxie said, "You probably have a lot of studying to do."

"Honestly, I do," Sabrina answered.

Roxie sat down at her desk and read over her psychology notes. After a few minutes she looked up at Sabrina and said, "On my way home I passed by a black cat and I could have sworn it was Salem. Was he here before?"

Sabrina had to answer. "Yes."

"I called him, but he ran in the other direction. He used to hang around all the time, but I haven't seen him since last week. You don't think he's scared of me, do you?"

"No, of course Salem isn't scared of you," said Sabrina, covering her mouth before she added that he used to have a crush on Roxie.

"Then why isn't he around anymore?"

"Oh, because I asked him not to come by. He was too much of a distraction. Too much of a pest." *Whoops,* thought Sabrina. She could have kicked herself!

"You asked a cat not to come by?" asked Roxie. "Don't you mean you asked your aunts not to let him out?"

"You like Salem," said Sabrina, speaking the first truth that came to mind—the first one that didn't reveal that Salem Saberhagen was a former witch.

"Well yeah, of course," said Roxie. "I like all animals—they're much nicer than humans."

"That's so sweet!" said Sabrina. Worried about getting into any more trouble, she turned out her reading light and got under her covers, hoping that Roxie would take that as a hint to stop asking her questions.

"You're already tired? It's so early," said Roxie.

Sabrina couldn't lie, so instead she pretended to snore.

That was fast, thought Roxie. She turned off the lights in the room and went outside to watch TV. "Sleep well," she whispered on her way out.

Once Roxie was gone, Sabrina threw the covers off her body in a huff. She was too stressed to sleep well. One small thought brought her some relief, however: At least Salem wasn't around. Surprisingly, he'd left when she'd asked him to. But what had he meant when he'd said, "You'll be seeing plenty of me soon enough"? She didn't know, but she had too much on her mind to give the matter much thought.

Not wanting to get too down about her latest snafu,

Sabrina reminded herself that things had been going well. Her workshop experience wasn't a complete disaster. At least Sabrina had written a poem that she was proud of. And she'd learned some things about honesty. For one, maybe it's not always best to hear the totally brutal and uncensored truth. Sure, she'd wanted opinions on her poetry, but perhaps she'd expected too much from the workshop. Obviously not everyone was there to give constructive feedback.

Sabrina decided that she'd try to get some sleep and, first thing in the morning, she'd pop over to her aunts' house to see if they might have any advice for her or, ideally, a way to remove the spell. And if they couldn't help her, well, she'd just hang out at their place until the spell wore off. She'd tell her housemates that she had a lot of work do to—it was the truth, so the spell would allow it. *Yes, this seems like a great plan,* thought Sabrina as she drifted off to sleep.

If only things had actually worked out that way.

Chapter 5

"Sabrina, your aunts are here!" called Morgan.

"Huh?" said Sabrina, stirred from her sleep early on Friday morning.

"Sabrina, it's much too early for company. I have my beauty sleep to think about. I'm going back to bed."

Sabrina sat up. Could it be? Had her aunts realized she was in trouble? Were they here to help her out? She was so happy, she leaped out of bed and ran for the door.

"Aunt Hilda, Aunt Zelda!" she cried, rushing out and giving them both big hugs. "I'm so happy to see you guys. You have no idea. I mean, maybe you do have an idea and that's why you're here! Woo-hoo!"

"What are you talking about?" asked Hilda.

It was then that Sabrina noticed Zelda was holding a carrying case. And in that carrying case was Salem.

Sabrina blinked and rubbed her eyes. Her aunts were both wearing big floppy straw hats. Even though it was only forty degrees out, they were in pastel shorts and tank tops. "You guys look like you're dressed for a cruise!" she said.

"Exactly." Zelda handed Salem to Sabrina and whispered, "We're going on a weeklong intergalactic cruise and you agreed to cat-sit for Salem, remember?"

"Uh-oh," said Sabrina.

"What's wrong?" asked Hilda.

Sabrina covered her mouth with one hand. She couldn't tell her aunts about the mess she was in. It would ruin their vacation. A vacation they'd been looking forward to for months. Sabrina had been so caught up with school and work and her latest mess, she'd forgotten all about agreeing to cat-sit.

"I think something's wrong with Sabrina," Hilda whispered to Zelda, loud enough for Sabrina to hear.

Sabrina grinned feebly, wishing she could assure them that there was nothing wrong with her at all. Of course, the Honesty Spell prevented her from doing this.

"Did you forget that you were supposed to cat-sit?" asked Zelda.

"Yes," Sabrina said in all honesty.

"Is it a problem?" asked Hilda.

"You know," said Sabrina, opening up Salem's cage and setting it down on the couch, "I was thinking about hiding out at your house all weekend. What if I brought Salem there? Wouldn't that be easier for everyone?" She grinned, realizing that once she got used to it, diverting the truth was kind of a snap, maybe even fun.

"Why do you say 'hiding out'?" asked Hilda. "That seems like a strange choice of words."

"You got a haircut!" said Sabrina, changing the subject as quickly as possible.

"I did." Hilda turned around and modeled the back of her head for Sabrina. "Do you like it?"

Sabrina's hand shot to her mouth because, actually, the cut was a bit uneven. When she recovered, she turned to Zelda. "So I can stay at your house, right?"

"I'm afraid not," said Zelda. Lowering her voice, she said, "Patricia is visiting."

"Patricia?" said Sabrina.

Zelda whispered in Sabrina's ear, "Patricia is a scientist from Ingraft—a small planet in a neighboring solar system. We've known one another for a hundred years. We studied together for our Ph.D.'s."

"Of course," Sabrina whispered. "Patricia is your friend who was once engaged to Salem when he was still a witch."

Zelda nodded sadly. "And he left her at the altar."

"There are two sides to every story," said Salem, leaping up onto the highest couch cushion and waving one paw.

"Yes, that's true," said Hilda, pushing him onto the floor. "There's a right side—and a horribly wrong, cruel, and unnecessary side."

Salem slinked off to the kitchen in search of some crumbs.

Sabrina grimaced, realizing that she was going to be stuck with Salem for an entire week. "And she never got over her heartbreak, right?"

"Yes," said Zelda. "Why, the last time I saw her, I couldn't even mention Salem's name without having her burst into tears."

"That's horrible," said Sabrina.

"No kidding," said Zelda. "And Patricia is an inventor working on an important project, the ingredients for which can be found only on Earth. She needs peace and quiet for a few days, and I'm afraid that with the distraction of Salem, it might render her incapable. This is very important, Sabrina."

Great, no pressure, thought Sabrina.

"So look, hon," said Hilda, interrupting. "If we don't shake a tail feather, we're going to miss the free welcome cocktails. And you know how I don't like to pass up a free cocktail."

"Okay," said Sabrina, smiling weakly.

"Are you sure this isn't a problem?" asked Zelda.

Sabrina covered her mouth with her hand before blurting out that, yes, as she saw it, Salem was going to be a huge problem.

"Hey, are you playing charades?" asked Hilda, pushing Zelda aside. "I love that game."

Eyes wide, Sabrina shook her head no.

"Okay, sounds like, what?" asked Hilda, tugging on her ear.

Sabrina stomped her foot, trying to signal to Hilda to cut it out.

"Thump," said Hilda, pointing. "You're thumping your foot. Sounds like *thump*. Wait—don't tell me. Lump? Clump? Stump?"

"No," said Sabrina. "I'm not playing charades."

"Then what are you doing?" asked Zelda.

Sabrina answered her with another truth. "You guys are going to be late if you don't hurry." She walked them to the front door.

"Okay," said Zelda. "Have fun. Don't forget to study!"

"We'll miss you," said Hilda.

"If you need anything, just call," said Zelda.

"Bye-bye," said Sabrina. Once the door was closed, though, she let out a whimper.

"So," said Salem, who had just knocked over Miles's box of Cocoa Krispies, "let's party!"

Sabrina turned to Salem, saying, "I can't deal with you right now."

"Geh?" asked Salem. "What did I ever do to you?"

"Where do I begin?" asked Sabrina as she scooped up Salem and brought him into her room. Luckily for her, Roxie was already gone.

"I didn't want to say that to you," she told him.

"Apology accepted," said Salem. "Are you hungry?"

Sabrina pointed and conjured up a bowl of tuna for Salem, if only to distract him while she tried to come up with a new plan. Part of her wanted to confess her problems to Salem. He was, after all, a former witch. Surely he'd have some idea how to help.

Salem smacked his lips and then burped loudly. "Now that's the kind of treatment I like!"

"Salem, I cast an honesty spell last night," Sabrina blurted out.

"Aha! That was one of my favorites," said Salem. "It was a great way to find out where the money was kept. First rule of domination, Sabrina, is follow the money."

"Yeah, whatever. Anyway, then I un-cast the spell a few minutes later," said Sabrina.

"What, are you crazy? Didn't you read the fine print?" asked Salem.

"No," said Sabrina. "I didn't even read the large print. I just winged it. Later, I looked it up and read all of the print, so now I know I have to be honest for"—she glanced at her watch—"well, I have about thirty-five hours to go."

"So that's why you don't want me around?"

"Well, you can be a pest sometimes," Sabrina said. Covering her mouth, she said, "I didn't mean to say that. It's true, of course, but I don't want to hurt your feelings."

"So now what? Wait, I think I know the drill. You want me to stay out of your hair until you can stop being so brutally honest?"

Sabrina smiled and scratched Salem behind the ears. "That would be so great. Thanks so much. I'm really glad you understand."

"Yeah, yeah, don't get mushy on me," said Salem.

Glancing at her clock, Sabrina realized she was almost late for history class. "Gotta go," she said.

"See ya," said Salem.

After Sabrina had grabbed her towel and headed for the bathroom, Salem let out an evil laugh.

"I said I'd stay out of your hair, Sabrina. But I never said anything about your housemates'! Oh, this is going to be so much fun!"

Chapter 6

Okay, Sabrina thought as she walked across campus to her history class. *I just have two classes to get through this morning. I can do this. I can be honest and not draw attention to myself.*

"Good morning Sabrina!" said Miles.

Startled, Sabrina looked up. "Yes, it is morning. Honestly. But what's so good about it?"

"Hey, relax," said Miles, throwing up his hands in mock-surrender. "You're starting to sound like me."

"I'm sorry. You just startled me. Are you going to Dr. Lethem's lecture now?"

"Indeed," said Miles, falling into step with Sabrina. "Can I walk you there, or are you going to bite my head off?"

"I'll try not to," said Sabrina. "And I want to apologize about what I said to you last night. It was insensitive and cruel—I didn't mean to blurt out that your jeans were too big." Sabrina was pleased that she'd been able to dance carefully around the issue of truth—that Miles's jeans were too big. She took it as a sign that she was actually going to be okay.

"It wouldn't have been a big deal except now Morgan is on this whole Let's-give-Miles-a-makeover kick," said Miles.

Sabrina followed him into the lecture hall, saying, "That could be dangerous." She almost added that Morgan's taste was not exactly what she would call good, but luckily she caught herself, covering her hand with her mouth before the truth escaped.

"Hey, can I borrow your copy of *The Prince*?" asked Miles as he took a seat toward the back of the room. "I think Machiavelli is going to show up on the midterm, and my copy disappeared."

"I think Salem probably took it."

"What are you talking about?" asked Miles. "Are you suggesting that your cat can read? I always thought he was strangely perceptive. But when it comes to animal intelligence, based on the studies I've read, I'd put my money on chimpanzees, hands down."

"So, Miles . . ." As Sabrina pulled her history

notebook out of her bag she changed the subject. "You also think that intelligent life can be found on other planets, right?"

"Of course," said Miles. "I actually have this new hypothesis I'm working on. It's sort of a companion to the Big Bang theory. You see, I believe there are clones somewhere out there in a parallel universe, and if we could just figure out a way to breathe without oxygen, then there'd be nothing stopping us from seeking them out."

"Really?" said Sabrina.

"Yes." Miles pushed his hair out of his face and looked at Sabrina quizzically. "I didn't know you were interested in this stuff."

"I'd like for you to keep talking," said Sabrina. If Miles chattered on, she wouldn't get a chance to slip up again.

Lucky for her, Miles was so wrapped up in his ideas that he was never suspicious. "That's good to hear, because with your investigative reporter skills and your connections to the media, I'll bet we could blow the whole cover right off this thing!"

Dr. Lethem walked into the room and called the class to attention before Sabrina could tell Miles she wasn't really interested in his theories and that she was only trying to distract him. Moreover, her "connections to the media" barely extended beyond her picking up coffee and doughnuts for real journalists.

"Please open up your history textbooks to page three hundred seventy-four," said Dr. Lethem, unbuttoning her navy blazer. She was a no-nonsense woman: tall, thin, and stern, with a posture that reminded Sabrina of a flagpole. "Now, who has an opinion on Theda Skocpol's theory of revolution?" She paced back and forth in front of her students, heels clicking on the linoleum floor, and looked around the room.

Fifty students looked elsewhere—at the ceiling, under their desks, down at their feet, or out the window. Since no one volunteered, Dr. Lethem called on someone randomly. That someone happened to be Sabrina. "Ms. Spellman, did you finish reading chapters twenty-two through twenty-five this week?"

Sabrina gulped and felt her face burn red. "No," she said. "I didn't get a chance to finish."

"Well, how much of the assignment did you read?" asked Dr. Lethem, somewhat taken aback. She had a reputation for being a professor with strict standards. If students didn't complete the reading, it wasn't beyond her to throw them out of class. But this young woman was being so honest. It was unacceptable but, at the same time, somewhat refreshing.

Sabrina sank down lower in her seat. She didn't want to admit that she'd only read the first few pages, but it wasn't like she could clamp her mouth shut and refuse to answer her professor. Taking a deep breath, she employed the diversion technique, quoting something she'd read in a book review. "Many people say that Theda Skocpol's theory of revolution is missing something important. She talks about structure, but doesn't allow for individual human action."

Dr. Lethem paced back and forth in front of the lecture room. "And do you agree with what many people say, Ms. Spellman?"

Sabrina shrugged. "I'm not really sure. I suppose I need to read more before I give my own opinion."

"Very well," said Dr. Lethem, seemingly impressed. "But may I suggest that if you want to pass this class, you do the reading?"

"Wow," said Sabrina, without thinking. "I'm surprised you didn't throw me out of class."

All eyes in the lecture room turned to Sabrina, who was now covering her mouth with both hands.

Luckily Dr. Lethem had a sense of humor. "You know, Ms. Spellman, I don't know if anyone's ever told you this, but there is such a thing as too much honesty."

Keeping her hands over her mouth, Sabrina nodded.

Meanwhile, back at her house, Salem happily tore through the kitchen pantry. "So much food, I don't know where to begin!" he said as he finished off Miles's tortilla chips, Morgan's rice cakes, and Roxie's pretzels.

Burping, he went back into Sabrina's room to use her computer. The month before, he'd met the most fascinating woman online—a surgeon from Bangladesh. They'd spent hours online instant messaging, which was no easy feat for Salem. It's hard typing with paws instead of fingers. Salem was thrilled with his newfound romance. He couldn't wait to get back in touch with Dr. Prentel. Especially since he'd just sent her a stunning picture of himself.

Salem leaped onto Sabrina's desk and, since he needed space to work, pushed all of her books and papers over the edge and onto the floor. Pressing the power button with one paw, he waited while the computer booted up. "Dr. Prentel, your dreams are about to come true!" he said as he swayed back and forth.

"Sabrina, is that you?" asked Morgan, bursting into Sabrina's room.

Looking around, all Morgan saw was Salem, blinking up at her innocently. "If Sabrina's not here, who was just talking?" She picked Salem up and stroked his fur.

Salem purred. *Oh yeah, baby,* he thought. *Now scratch behind my ears.*

"Did you make that mess in the kitchen?" Morgan asked.

"Meow!" he said, in his best house cat accent.

Morgan noticed that Sabrina's computer was on. "Did you do that? Oh Salem, you don't want to play in here. Come on." She carried him out of the bedroom and closed the door behind her.

Salem sighed. All of his hard work was for nothing.

Morgan opened up a can of cat food for Salem and set it down on the ground.

He looked from the can of food to Morgan, thinking, *You expect me to eat that?*

"What's wrong?" Morgan cooed. "It's chicken

liver flavored. Cats love chicken liver–flavored stuff."

That's what you think, thought Salem, bending over the can unhappily and pretending to eat. The smell was making him nauseated. He looked up at Morgan, who was preparing her lunch.

Salem couldn't help but drool as he watched Morgan make herself a sandwich of sun-dried tomato, eggplant, and mozzarella cheese with pesto mayonnaise on his favorite kind of bread—focaccia. Oh the torture!

Please just drop one crumb, he tried to tell her with his eyes.

Morgan felt Salem's small yellow eyes boring into her, and it creeped her out—big time. Shuddering, she said, "Geez, it's almost like you know exactly what's going on here." She carried her sandwich up to her room, slamming the door in Salem's face when he tried to follow.

Salem went back downstairs. Since Sabrina's bedroom door was closed, he had to leap out the living room window, scamper around the house to Sabrina's bedroom window, and enter through there.

The computer hummed idlly on the desk. Salem started to approach, but then changed his mind. "On second thought," he said to himself, "maybe I'll just call Dr. Prentel in Bangladesh."

He knocked the receiver off the cradle of the phone and dialed. A few moments later, he'd made the connection. The phone was ringing. Salem was so happy! Zelda and Hilda had caught him running up their phone bill a few days ago, and had responded by creating a special code that had to be dialed before one could call long distance—a code that Salem hadn't managed to crack yet. But apparently in their haste to get ready for their vacation they'd forgotten to warn Sabrina. And this opened up a whole new world of possibilities.

"Dr. Prentel, please," Salem said when he heard a voice at the other end of the line.

"This is she," said the voice.

"Wow, you sound even sexier than I'd imagined," said Salem, happy that he hadn't lost his touch with the ladies.

"Who's calling?" Dr. Prentel asked suspiciously.

"Just the man you've been dreaming about for months."

"Who?" said Dr. Prentel.

"Salem Saberhagen," said Salem.

"You, Salem, have a lot of nerve!"

"What do you mean?" asked Salem, taken aback.

"I asked you to send me a picture of yourself," said Dr. Prentel.

"And . . ."

"I wanted a picture of you," she said, "not of Freddie Prinze Jr.! Is this a joke to you?"

"No joke," said Salem. "He's my twin!"

"I pour my heart and soul out to you and you mock?" said Dr. Prentel. "Unacceptable. I don't ever want to hear from you again!"

"Geh?" asked Salem. But he was talking to a dial tone. "Well," he said, hanging up the phone and turning to the computer, "watch out, ladies! Looks like Salem Saberhagen is back on the market."

Just then Salem heard a door slam and the unmistakable voice of Miles shout out, "Anyone home?"

Mortals, thought Salem. *Wait a minute. I can have some fun here.* With a mischievous grin painted on his small black face, he leaped out Sabrina's bedroom window. Entering the house through the living room window, he hid underneath the couch.

After an intense afternoon of class, and then three hours of playing video games at the local arcade,

Miles was starving. Making his way toward the kitchen he noticed that his box of Cocoa Krispies was knocked over. Peering inside, he realized it was empty. "Oh no," he said. "Well, I guess I'll just have to settle for some chips and dip." He found his bag of tortilla chips at the back of the kitchen pantry, but of course, it was empty. "Or just dip," said Miles, searching for a clean spoon. Finding none, he went to the phone and ordered a pizza. "Please hurry," he told the guy who answered the phone at Sergio's. It's an emergency."

Miles hung up the phone and picked up the remote. Before he turned on the TV, he heard a small voice say, "Miles!"

Miles froze. "Hello?" he said, looking to his right and left. He knocked on Sabrina and Roxie's door and, when no one answered, he peered inside. "Did someone say something?"

"Maybe," said Salem, with a mischievous snicker.

"Okay," said Miles, taking a few deep breaths and walking back to the couch. "I have control over this. I am not hearing things. Dr. Winters said it was all in my head."

"If only that were true," Salem added from under the couch.

"I'm just going to count to ten and clear my head and the voice will be gone." Miles tried to remain calm, but he could feel his heart pounding in his chest.

"No it won't," said Salem.

"One, two," Miles started.

"Buckle my shoe," said Salem.

Miles covered his ears with his hands and continued. "Three, four, five, six."

"I know that one. Pick up sticks."

Miles jumped up from the couch and ran out the door, much to Salem's dismay. "You could have left me some cash for the pizza!" Salem called.

Now what? wondered Salem. Scampering back to Sabrina's room through the door Miles had accidentally left open, Salem curled up on Roxie's pillow and took a nap.

Sabrina raced home that afternoon as soon as her last class was over. She took a different route in hopes that she wouldn't run into anyone she knew, and it worked. But much to her disappointment, once she got home she found Morgan on the living room couch, flipping through the pages of a fashion magazine.

"Hey Sabrina. I'm glad you're back," she said.

"You're coming to the Delta Tau Delta party tonight, right?"

"I don't think this weekend is a great time for me to be among mortals," said Sabrina.

"Oh," said Morgan, "you're still on that weird I'm-an-artist kick, huh?"

"No, I've hung up my pen," said Sabrina. "I'm just going to hole up all weekend and study."

"It's your life," said Morgan with a sigh, turning the page. "Your choice not to have one, that is."

"Right, thanks," said Sabrina on her way to her room.

"But I have to talk to you about something else," said Morgan.

"Are you still upset about my shoe comment?" asked Sabrina.

"No," said Morgan. "I don't care about that anymore. It's Salem who's bothering me."

"What did he do?" asked Sabrina, fearing the worst.

"Well, I think he's acting out. The kitchen was an absolute mess when I got home. And he hasn't touched his cat food. The poor little guy—he must be starving!"

"Where is the cute little guy right now?" asked

Sabrina through gritted teeth, straining to keep a smile on her face.

"I don't know. Last I saw him he was actually in front of your computer. That's before I took him out and fed him, that is," said Morgan. "But do you know why he's not eating? Do you think he's confused with your aunts away?"

"I think Salem knows exactly what he's doing," said Sabrina, trying to sneak into her room before she gave anything away.

"Hey, where did your aunts go, again?" asked Morgan, flipping her hair over her shoulder.

"On a cruise," said Sabrina.

"I love cruises!" said Morgan. "Where did they go? The Caribbean? The South Pacific? Alaska?"

"It's an intergalactic cruise," Sabrina said offhandedly. Then, realizing what had happened, she covered her mouth.

"Intergalactic?" said Morgan. "I've never heard of that company. Is that supposed to be better than a Carnival or Princess cruise?"

"I've had a really stressful day. I'm going to my room now."

Morgan looked at Sabrina questioningly, but before she could comment, Sabrina slipped into her room and closed the door behind her.

Noticing a familiar feline over at Roxie's stereo, she yelled, "Salem!"

"You called?" said Salem as he did the moonwalk across Roxie's desk in time to the music. He was wearing a pair of sunglasses, which Sabrina pointed away, into thin air.

"Did you mess up the kitchen and eat all of my housemates' food?" she asked.

"Hey, you're the one under the Honesty Spell. I don't have to admit to anything. In fact, I take the Fifth, and if you have anything else to say to me, then call my lawyer."

Sabrina turned off Roxie's stereo and put her CDs back in order. "Roxie's stuff is totally off limits. You know she's going to blame me, and it's not like I'm in a state to take the rap!"

"Because otherwise you'd be happy to?" said Salem.

"Because I'd have no choice. Come on, Salem. I thought you understood the position I was in."

"Oh, what's the big deal?" said Salem, turning on the stereo once more.

Sabrina turned it off and pointed at Salem—levitating him from Roxie's bed to the windowsill.

"Roxie has got lousy taste in music, anyway," said Salem, trying to maintain a thread of dignity. "The Smiths? The Cure? Please—Goth is so nineties!"

"Late eighties, really," said Sabrina, annoyed that Salem was making fun of her friend's taste in music. Despite this, however, Sabrina couldn't help but agree. Looking at one of the CDs, she said, "It's not my favorite genre either. Sometimes I think the depressing music Roxie listens to really influences her personality. In an unhealthy negative way, I mean."

"You're dissing me to your cat!" yelled Roxie, who had just stepped into their room in time to hear the tail end of their conversation.

"It's not like it looks," said Sabrina. "He started it." Sabrina covered her mouth with her hands, lest even more damaging truths escape.

"Do you think I like all of your music?" asked Roxie. "Let me tell you, I don't. But I wouldn't go talking about you behind your back. Especially to a pet. That's so uncool!"

"You're right," said Sabrina. "It wasn't a nice thing to do. I'm so sorry. I wish I could take it back."

"Whatever," said Roxie, turning around and leaving the room.

Once she was gone, Sabrina spun around to Salem, who was pretending to sleep. "I know you're faking," she said. "You probably think this is funny!"

Salem sighed. "Look, my girlfriend just dumped me. I have to amuse myself somehow."

"I'm not even going to ask, but do me this one small favor—try to act like a normal cat. At least until this spell wears off."

"Are you sure that's what you want?" asked Salem.

"Absolutely," said Sabrina. "That means no listening to music, no using the computer, no eating Cocoa Krispies, and—"

"Hey, easy on the rules," Salem said, cutting her off. "Remember, I'm a houseguest."

"I wasn't done," said Sabrina. "No talking. Please, I'm begging you."

"A lot of fun you turned out to be!" Salem said with a huff.

Sabrina pointed her finger, threateningly.

"What? I didn't do anything?" said Salem, his hair standing on ends because he was a bit freaked out. "Not another word from me, I promise. I'll start acting like a normal cat—now."

Sabrina let out a breath in relief. "Thank you."

"Meeow!" said Salem.

Sabrina scratched Salem behind the ears, and said, "That's a good little kitty." She was happy that Salem had agreed to go along with her little plan, but the truth was, Sabrina didn't believe him. It's not that she didn't think he wanted to behave—she just didn't think it was possible for him. It wasn't in his nature.

The whole situation was driving Sabrina crazy. Being around Salem was dangerous. Thinking about her morning on campus, Sabrina realized that she'd been okay on her own. Sure, there'd been some awkward moments. But she'd been able to think on her toes, come up with excuses, and smooth over most situations. Perhaps it would be better for Sabrina to get away from Salem for a while—before she lost her mind. And since Salem would be at Sabrina's all night, she decided she'd go out.

She found Roxie and Morgan in the living room. Morgan had moved onto filing her fingernails, and Roxie was making a bowl of pasta.

"Hey Morgan?" said Sabrina.

"Yes?" Morgan looked up.

"Is the invitation still open? For that Delta Tau Delta party, I mean?"

"Totally," said Morgan. "I'm so glad you've had a change of heart."

"Yeah," said Sabrina. "Me too. I think getting out of this house is just what I need to do."

Just then Miles stormed into the house. He'd gone for a long walk to clear his head, and was feeling better. Now he had a new bone to pick. Catching Sabrina off guard, he asked. "Did you eat my Cocoa Krispies?"

"No," said Sabrina, in all honesty. "It wasn't me, it was Salem!"

Miles put his hands on his hips. "You're going to stand there and tell me that a cat ate my cereal?"

"Yes," said Sabrina meekly.

"You know, my rice cakes were missing today too," said Morgan. "Are you going to blame Salem?"

"Yes," said Sabrina, realizing how guilty she looked to them.

"What if we say we don't believe you?" asked Miles.

"I'd have to tell you you're wrong. I'm telling the truth. I can't help but tell the truth." Sabrina covered her mouth and ran into her room. She was hoping for some relief, but the scene she walked in on was even more irritating. "What are you doing?" she yelled.

"Huh?" Salem looked up from the stockings he was shredding.

"I can't believe you did this!" said Sabrina, holding up her favorite pair of stockings, the ones she was going to wear to the fraternity party that night—in fact, the only ones she had.

"You're the one who told me to act like a normal cat," said Salem, looking too pleased with himself.

"I can't believe you did this," yelled Sabrina. Since she forgot to close her bedroom door, her voice drifted out into the living room.

Seconds later, Miles, Morgan, and Roxie were in her room.

"You're yelling at Salem again?" said Roxie, picking up the cat and giving him a cuddle. "Poor guy. Is the big, bad Sabrina giving you a hard time?"

"What's the big deal?" asked Morgan. "Why are you acting like such a spaz?"

"Those were my last pair of stockings," said Sabrina. "I was going to wear them to the party tonight."

"He's just a cat," said Miles. "He doesn't know any better. And if he did, I'm sure he'd be upset that you were blaming him for eating all of our food."

"This is hopeless," said Sabrina, throwing up her hands in frustration. "He's not just a cat. He's—" Covering her mouth, Sabrina sprinted for the bathroom. Once inside, she slammed and locked the door, then flushed the toilet so no one could hear her say, "Salem Saberhagen is a conniving former witch!"

Chapter 7

Sabrina decided she was done playing Ms. Nice Witch. If Salem wasn't going to help her out on her terms, she was going to have to switch over to his.

"Hee, hee, hee . . ." She imitated Salem's evil laugh as she looked around to make sure she was alone. She pointed at the oven, took out a fully cooked and delicious-smelling lasagna, and finally pointed up a new outfit for tonight's party.

"What are you doing?" asked Salem, hopping up onto the counter.

"No talking," she reminded him.

"Don't worry, I've got everyone covered. Morgan's in the shower. Roxie's listening to music with her headphones on, and Miles is on the phone with a psychic hotline."

"Great," said Sabrina sarcastically. "And it's not like this would be the first time they caught me talking to you."

"And you're suggesting that this is my fault because . . ."

"Never mind," said Sabrina.

"So what are you doing? And you have to answer me because I know you're under that spell for another twenty-four hours."

Sabrina glared at Salem, annoyed that he was getting so much pleasure out of her latest mess. "I'm making dinner for my wonderful housemates."

"Great, it smells delicious!" said Salem, smacking his lips. "For the first time all day, I'm glad to be an honorary guest."

"And for you," said Sabrina, pointing to the counter and zapping up a bag of dried cat food. "I have this!"

Salem leaned away from the food and shuddered. "You're not suggesting . . ."

Grinning, Sabrina nodded.

"Hilda and Zelda would never feed me cat food!"

"Aunt Hilda and Aunt Zelda," Sabrina reminded Salem, "are on Neptune."

"You're doing this on purpose!" Salem cried.

"You're right," said Sabrina, cutting the lasagna into squares. "And I'm loving it!"

"What's cooking?" asked Miles, coming out of his bedroom.

"Lasagna. I made us all dinner," said Sabrina. "I ran out and went grocery shopping. I picked you up some more Cocoa Krispies, lactose-free milk, and, since I noticed you were out of tortilla chips, I got some of those, too."

Miles's eyes lit up. "You did that for me?"

"Yes," said Sabrina.

"You're amazing, Sabrina. It seems like just an hour ago you were coming home from classes. I don't know how you managed to go shopping and make this great dinner. I thought you were in your room this whole time!"

"Ha-ha," said Sabrina.

"No, seriously," said Miles. "How did you do it?"

"I used magic." Sabrina shrugged her shoulders as if it were the most natural thing in the world.

Assuming she was joking, Miles shook his head and grinned. "You must have."

"Right—anyway, let's eat." Sabrina walked to the bottom of the staircase. "Morgan!"

"I'm doing my hair!" yelled Morgan.

"I made lasagna!" said Sabrina.

Morgan appeared at the top of the steps half a second later. "Be right down."

Sabrina went into her room to get Roxie. "I made a peace offering," she said once Roxie had slipped her headphones off her ears.

"Huh?" said Roxie.

"I'm sorry I've been acting weird. Weirder than usual, that is," said Sabrina. "It's been kind of a crazy time. I wish I could tell you about it, but if I did, it would put you in mortal danger and I'll probably end up losing my powers."

"This is your idea of an apology?" asked Roxie, more confused by Sabrina's behavior than before.

"Sorry," Sabrina said with a grin. "The apology is in the kitchen. I made everyone lasagna. And I replaced your pretzels."

"My pretzels were missing?" asked Roxie.

"Yes," said Sabrina. "But please don't ask why."

Roxie followed Sabrina out into the common area, where Miles had set the table.

After pouring Salem some of his much-dreaded dry cat food, Sabrina dished up lasagna for Roxie, Miles, and Morgan.

"This is great," said Morgan.

"You're an amazing cook," said Miles, his cheeks stuffed full of food.

"It almost makes up for your crazy behavior," said Roxie.

Salem whimpered, thinking, *This cat food tastes like chalk!*

Sabrina sighed and, looking straight at Salem, said, "It is quite delicious, isn't it?"

"So," said Morgan, finishing first and clearing her plate. "Who wants to come with me and Sabrina to the Delta Tau Delta party?"

"I'll pass," said Roxie. "I need to rearrange my sock drawer tonight."

"I'm out too," said Miles. "It's such a clear night—perfect for stargazing. I can't pass that up. Especially since I have this great new high-power lens."

"Okay," said Morgan. "Sabrina, I'm just going to run upstairs and reapply my lipstick. You're not going to take too long to get dressed, are you?"

Sabrina looked down at herself, stunned. She was wearing a pair of black pants and a silver tank—an outfit that she thought would be perfect for the party. Well, her blue miniskirt would have been more perfect—but since Salem shredded her stockings and all of her housemates heard her yell that they were her last pair, she couldn't point up another without looking suspicious. "I'm already dressed," she said to Morgan.

"Oh! I'm sorry," said Morgan. "To each her own."

"You know, sometimes you can be too much," said Sabrina, regretting the words immediately after she said them. Luckily for her, though, Morgan had been examining her eyelashes in the reflection of the toaster oven and hadn't even been paying attention.

Twenty minutes later they entered the pulsating throng that was the party. College students crammed together in the basement of the fraternity house. The floor was sticky. The music was loud, and the conversations were louder. Stray bits of information floated over to where Sabrina stood.

"Crazy week. . . . How did you do on the French midterm? I used to think he was great, but then I got to know him. . . . Love those jeans. . . . Am so glad it's over. . . . Did you see Dr. Sentsia in the student center? Cute shoes. . . . I'm going to ask her tonight. . . ."

Sabrina blinked and rubbed her temples. She was starting to get a headache. Even though she wasn't with Salem, she couldn't help but worry. Now that he wasn't under her surveillance, was he doing even more damage at the house?

Morgan smiled and shouted to Sabrina, "This is the best party! Don't you think?"

"To be honest with you," said Sabrina, "no. I was just trying to figure out why I bothered coming."

Morgan put her hands on her hips. "Nice attitude! What is with you?"

"I'm sorry," said Sabrina. "I had to tell you the truth. I'd rather make something up, believe me."

"You're acting really weird," said Morgan. Standing up on her tiptoes she surveyed the crowd and recognizing her TA from her sociology class. "That guy is so cute."

Sabrina looked over. "You're right. He's pretty cute."

"Okay," said Morgan. "I'm going in for the kill. How do I look?" She flashed Sabrina a dazzling smile.

"Great, but you have a bit of lipstick on your front tooth," said Sabrina.

"Oh, my gosh—you are a lifesaver!" Morgan wiped off the lipstick and asked again. "Okay now?"

"Great," said Sabrina. "And I really like that

shade of red. Good luck." She watched Morgan make her way across the room and sighed.

Turning around, she saw a tall and thin guy with blond hair and a pale complexion standing before her. "I know you," she said, pointing, not quite able to place him.

"Jason. I was in Max's poetry workshop," he said with a lopsided grin.

"Of course," said Sabrina. "That was really smart of you—not to show up last week."

"What do you mean?" asked Jason.

Sabrina clamped her hand over her mouth, lest she say anything incriminating or unkind. And since he was still standing there staring at her, she stated the obvious in hopes of diverting his question. "So this is a pretty loud party."

"Tell me about it," said Jason, glancing over his shoulder.

The party was so loud that Sabrina didn't hear his reply. "What?" she asked.

Jason repeated himself, this time shouting over the noise.

"Do you go to Adams?" she asked.

"Yes."

"Me too," said Sabrina. "When did you get here?"

"About a year and a half ago," said Jason.

"Huh?" asked Sabrina.

"I live here," Jason said, with the wave of one hand. "In this house, I mean, not in this room."

"Luckily," said Sabrina, noticing that someone had just inadvertently knocked over a bowl of potato chips. No one nearby seemed to notice, and the crowd was stomping all over the chips, grinding the tiny crumbs into the carpet.

"No kidding. Are you having fun?" asked Jason.

Sabrina was in a bind: She had to answer, but she didn't want to hurt Jason's feelings. It was his fraternity house, after all. Would he be insulted if she admitted she wasn't having a good time? Sabrina took a deep breath and decided to take the risk. "No," she said. "To be honest, I'm not."

"Wow," said Jason, smiling to reveal dimples. "That's so refreshing to hear. I'm not having a good time either. Want to go outside for some air?"

"Definitely," said Sabrina.

"Follow me," said Jason as he turned and weaved his way through the crowd.

Sabrina noticed Morgan dancing with her TA in the center of the room. She waved as she passed her, and Morgan, tossing her hair over her shoulder, smiled.

A few moments later, Jason and Sabrina were outside, in blissful near-silence. They could still hear the noise from the party, but the deafening roar had mellowed to a gentle lull.

The night was cool, but pleasantly so. "This is so much better," Sabrina said. She meant it too. She could already feel her headache fading away.

"No kidding." Jason sat down on the porch swing and said, "So why—"

Sabrina cut him off, deciding that the safest thing for her, given the spell, would be to keep asking questions. "So why weren't you at the workshop last week?"

"I wanted to go. I even finished a draft of a poem, but then I got caught up in this whole other mess."

"What mess?" asked Sabrina, interested in what he had to say and interested in keeping him talking.

"Tell me about the workshop first. How did it go?"

"I spent so many hours on my poem," said Sabrina truthfully. "It's all kind of a blur."

Jason readjusted his baseball cap. "I'll bet it was really great."

Sabrina shook her head. "It was totally anticlimactic."

"You mean because you worked so hard and your

moment of glory was over in a few seconds?" asked Jason.

"Not exactly," said Sabrina, not really worried, for some reason, that she was unguarded. Jason seemed to be the kind of guy she could be totally honest with. "Max turned out to be a total phony. And the person who liked my poem the most totally misinterpreted it."

Jason nodded and frowned. "Sounds awful."

"Yeah," said Sabrina. "So what happened that you couldn't go to the workshop?"

Jason sighed. "It's a long story. Are you sure you want to hear it?"

Sabrina nodded. "I'd love to hear it. The longer the better—just keep talking!"

"Well, I was trying to track down our fraternity's mascot."

"I didn't know fraternities had mascots."

"They don't always," said Jason. "But we do—I mean, we did."

"What was it?"

Jason frowned. "A miniature donkey. His name was Goldie."

"That's so cute," said Sabrina.

"Goldie was great. He was like a fixture in this

house. The fraternity had had him for a few years. I was in charge of feeding him this term."

"Isn't it hard to have a miniature donkey in Boston?" asked Sabrina.

"We sent him to a farm in the winter. And there was always someone willing to take him home for the summer. I had him last year. My parents have a pretty big yard in upstate New York, so it was never a problem."

"So what happened?" asked Sabrina.

"Someone sold Goldie on eBay," said Jason sadly.

"You're kidding! That's horrible."

"I know. A lot of the guys—they didn't like Goldie. They thought she was too much of a bother. And the house had gone through our savings in the first few months. Without money, we couldn't throw any more parties." Jason glanced over his shoulder toward the house. "So they decided that Goldie would have to go."

"I'm so sorry," said Sabrina, already trying to come up with ways in which she could help.

"I grew up with animals my whole life. Dogs, cats, ferrets, hamsters, goldfish—you name it, at some point I had it. But Goldie was special. He was like a friend. And how can you auction off a friend?"

Sabrina shook her head. "I couldn't imagine."

"Are you an animal lover?" asked Jason.

Sabrina laughed, thinking about Salem's antics and her frustrations. "For the most part."

"What do you mean?" asked Jason.

Sabrina sighed as she considered her options. She could clamp her hand over her mouth and run for cover, bring up some new absurd truth to divert Jason, or just tell him the truth. Since she was having a good time talking to him, and since he was being so sincere with her, she chose the latter. "I'm cat-sitting for my aunts and I'm really having a hard time."

"How come?" asked Jason.

"Salem—that's the cat's name—he gets into everything. He's eaten all my housemates' food, for one thing." Sabrina decided to quit while she was ahead. She turned to Jason and asked him something innocuous. "So, who are your favorite poets?"

Jason kicked at the ground with his sneaker and, much to Sabrina's chagrin, ignored her question. "Is Salem acting up worse than usual?"

"He's always been kind of a pest," said Sabrina.

"But he and my aunts Hilda and Zelda, they fight like . . . well, like cats and dogs. I know it sounds crazy, but Salem seems to get pleasure out of giving me a hard time. Probably because I live with mortals—college students, I mean." Sabrina could kick herself!

"How old is he?" asked Jason.

"A few hundred years old," said Sabrina, covering her mouth a little too late.

"Yeah, cats live forever," said Jason, nodding, assuming she was stretching the truth for effect.

"You have no idea."

"I'll bet I could help," said Jason.

Sabrina asked, "How so?"

"Well, the house just isn't the same without a mascot. What if we adopted Salem for the rest of the term?"

"Thanks for the offer, but that wouldn't work," said Sabrina. "He's not mine, and my aunts would never go for that. Salem is such a handful, you really don't want to get involved, trust me."

"How long are you cat-sitting for?" asked Jason.

"Until next Friday," said Sabrina.

"Well," said Jason. "What if I took Salem off your hands until then?"

Sabrina flashed Jason a sideways glance. "I don't

get it. Why would you want Salem for just a few days?"

"I think if I bring him to the house and convince the guys how great it is to have an animal around—how we really need to have a mascot—then we all win. You don't have to worry about the cat, and eventually the house will get a new mascot. Maybe we can even get Goldie back."

"Hmm . . . Salem living in a house full of Adams College fraternity guys . . . I don't know about that," said Sabrina.

"Think about it," said Jason.

Sabrina shook her head. "Letting Salem out of my sight for too long is dangerous, trust me."

"Okay," said Jason, trying to hide his disappointment.

"Thanks for trying to help, though. I know you mean well."

Jason shrugged. "It's okay."

Sabrina looked at her watch. "Speaking of Salem, I should probably get back home and see what kind of damage he's done."

"Want me to walk you?" asked Jason.

"Sure," Sabrina said with a smile. "Let me just check on Morgan."

Sabrina walked back into the party and pushed

past Adams College coeds until she found Morgan, who was still dancing. "I'm taking off."

"What?" yelled Morgan.

"I'm going home now," Sabrina shouted.

"But it's so early," said Morgan.

"I'll see you later." Sabrina waved and then went back outside, where Jason was waiting for her.

As they walked they looked up at the sky. Miles had been right when he said it was the perfect night for stargazing. The sky was a beautiful shade of dark blue—almost navy, but not quite. The stars were clear and stunning.

"That's Orion's belt," said Jason, pointing to a chain of three stars.

"I know," said Sabrina, smiling, realizing her aunts were scheduled to cruise by there that very night.

"Did you take astronomy with Dr. Fletcher too?"

"No," said Sabrina. "But I know my way around the solar system."

"How come?" asked Jason.

"My aunts took me on a trip there for my seventeenth birthday," said Sabrina.

"Huh?" asked Jason.

"Oh," Sabrina said, realizing she'd just backed

herself into a corner. "I mean, hey, that's a nice house, huh? I really like Tudors."

"Sure," said Jason, thoroughly confused.

Sabrina picked up the pace, wishing she hadn't agreed to let Jason walk her home. The Honesty Spell could really get her into trouble. "There's Cassiopeia!" she said, pointing up at the sky.

"Yeah, I missed that one on the final," said Jason.

"So are you going to go back to Max's workshop?" Sabrina asked.

"Definitely. I just hope he's not too upset that I bailed when I was supposed to read my poem last week."

"I think he has other things on his mind," said Sabrina. "I wouldn't worry about it at all."

When they approached Sabrina's house, Salem was waiting for them on the porch swing.

"Hey Salem," said Sabrina. "This is Jason."

Jason bent down to pet Salem on the top of his head. "He's got a great coat of fur."

"Don't say that too loudly," Sabrina said with a smirk. "He's quite vain."

Salem purred loudly and melodramatically.

"You're so cute," said Jason, cupping Salem's face in his two hands.

It was clear to Sabrina that Jason wasn't kidding when he said he was an animal lover.

Salem started to growl, so Jason backed off.

"So, Jason. Thanks for walking me home," said Sabrina.

"No problem," said Jason. "I'll see you next Thursday at the workshop?"

"Probably not," said Sabrina. "I've had some second thoughts about the whole poetry thing."

"That's too bad," said Jason.

Sabrina shrugged, not knowing what else to say.

"Are you having second thoughts about letting us borrow Salem?" asked Jason.

"Geh?" said Salem.

Sabrina shot Salem a look that told him not to say another word. Taking his cue, he scampered back into the house through the open window.

Turning back to Jason, Sabrina shook her head. "Believe me, I'd love to get Salem off my hands for a while. It would make my life a lot easier. But it just wouldn't work."

"Okay," said Jason with a shrug. "But if you change your mind, you know where to find me."

"I sure do," said Sabrina. "Thanks for walking me home. It was really nice to get to know you."

"I'll see you around," said Jason. Hands in his pockets, he backed up, turned, and then walked away.

"Someone's got a crush!" Salem sang to Sabrina as soon as she walked into the house.

"Shh!" she said, raising her finger to her lips. "Someone's going to hear you."

"Roxie is sleeping, and Miles left," said Salem.

"Miles left?" asked Sabrina. "Where did he go?"

"I think he went to the hospital. He was scared."

"What happened?"

Salem shrugged.

"Salem, what did you do? I thought we had an agreement," Sabrina cried.

"We did," said Salem. "The agreement was that I'd stay out of your hair. I never said anything about your housemates'."

"And shredding my last pair of stockings is your idea of staying out of my hair?" asked Sabrina.

"You told me to act like a normal cat," said Salem. "I was improvising."

"Normal cats do not taunt people. Normal cats do not have an answer for everything," said Sabrina.

"Now you're sending me mixed messages," said Salem. "How am I supposed to react? You're making things very difficult."

Sabrina, having lost all of her patience, was momentarily speechless. The night had been too stressful. And coming home to Salem—it was too much. Suddenly Sabrina's headache was back.

"Who is that clown, anyway?" Salem asked.

"He's not a clown. I met him in my poetry workshop, and the party was at his fraternity house tonight. He's got very cute dimples." Sabrina covered her mouth, but it was too late. The truth had escaped, and now Salem had plenty of material with which to tease her.

"You do have a crush!" he said. "I knew it. Can I call these things or what?"

"I should have given you away to Jason!" said Sabrina.

Salem gasped. "You considered giving me away?"

"Don't I wish," Sabrina said.

"Geh!"

"Look, Salem. To be honest—as if I had a choice—you're just too much of a handful. It would be okay if we were at my aunts' house. But here, between my schoolwork, living with mortals, and this Honesty Spell, having to watch your every move is totally exhausting."

"Way to make a cat feel welcome," Salem said sarcastically.

Sabrina wished she could take back what she'd said. "I'm sorry," she told him. "If I hadn't been under this spell I wouldn't have had to put it to you in those terms exactly."

"What does that matter if that's how you really feel?"

"It matters because I don't like hurting anyone's feelings," said Sabrina. "Even the feelings of a somewhat conniving former witch."

"Is that all I am to you?" asked Salem.

Before Sabrina could answer him, Miles came home. He walked into the house slowly, with his head hanging down.

"You're back," said Sabrina. "Are you feeling okay?"

"Apparently," said Miles, sounding exhausted. "Health Services couldn't find anything wrong with me."

"That's good. I'm sure you're totally healthy." Sabrina couldn't help but add, "Aside from the everyday paranoid neurotic hypochondriac stuff, that is."

"Thanks," said Miles, slumping down onto the couch. "Do you know where the remote is?"

Salem pushed the remote control toward Miles with his paw.

"That's so weird," said Miles. "Do you think your cat understands what we're saying?"

"Um, let's make some popcorn," said Sabrina, changing the subject.

"You know, Sabrina, I think I should go to bed."

Once Miles was in his room, Sabrina pointed Salem outside.

Salem tried to crawl back inside, but he couldn't. Even though there was nothing in his way, every time he tried to enter the house through the window he felt like he was ramming his head into a brick wall.

"I put a spell on the house," Sabrina explained to him a few moments later when she managed to slip outside. "I need a break, so you are banned from entering until sunrise tomorrow."

"That's cruel!" said Salem.

"Considering what you've been up to for the past couple of days," said Sabrina, "I would say you're getting off easy."

"Hey, wait a minute!" yelled Salem.

But it was too late. Sabrina had closed the door on Salem, in all senses of the word.

"Meow!" Salem called.

Sabrina stuck her head out the window. "Please keep your voice down. Miles is in a very fragile state."

"What would your aunts say about how you're treating me?" asked Salem.

"They'd probably say that it was long overdue," said Sabrina, closing the window, happy that in this instance, speaking the bitter truth was actually appropriate.

Chapter 8

Salem collapsed on the porch swing in a fit of exhaustion and hunger. *Now what am I supposed to do?* he wondered.

The wind had changed direction, and the distinct scent of pepperoni pizza drifted Salem's way—answering his question. Ears perked and nose raised, he sniffed the air. "I think I smell a snack," he said before hopping off the porch and heading down the street.

Salem turned right at the corner and then continued down the block. Crossing the street he leaped out of the way as a truck careened down the road. He managed to dodge it at the last second, but the tire hit a puddle, soaking the poor cat. Salem dried himself off by rolling around on a nearby front lawn. He cut through someone's backyard and then saw it in the distance: the pizza. Or, to be more specific, the crumpled pizza box. Salem approached the food. It was on the front porch of a fraternity house. A party was going on, full swing. Music blared and the sounds of laughter trickled out through the window, but none of this deterred Salem. He pounced, landing on the top step of the porch, scrambled toward the box, and pushed it open. There was one slice of pepperoni left. *Perfect!* Salem thought as he dove right in.

So consumed by his meal, Salem didn't hear the creak of the porch door as it swung open.

Jason was just stepping outside, trying to clear his head, wishing that everyone would go home so he could get some sleep. He missed Goldie horribly, and was still angry with his fraternity brothers for auctioning her off. He was also surprised by what he found on his porch. "Salem, is that you?" he asked, assuming that Sabrina had changed her mind.

Salem muffled a "Geh?" as he was scooped up, before he had finished half the slice.

Meanwhile, Sabrina lay in her bed staring at the glowing green numbers of her clock, which read 2:00 A.M. Eighteen hours and twenty minutes of honesty left to go, she calculated. A gentle breeze caused the trees to rustle outside. Someone's wind chimes were ringing faintly. She could tell from the sounds of Roxie's even breathing that her housemate was sleeping soundly. Sabrina couldn't help but be a little envious, because she was having trouble falling asleep.

Thinking she might as well use the time productively, she tried to study for history class, but she couldn't concentrate. She picked up a Gabriel García Márquez novel, but couldn't focus on that, either. Something was bothering her, but she wasn't quite sure what it was.

With Salem out of the picture and everyone she knew asleep, Sabrina should have had nothing to worry about. She'd managed to get through the day without having to spill the awful truth, and she'd hardly used any magic. Surely Saturday wouldn't be a problem. She could hole up in her room with her schoolbooks, avoiding her housemates and maybe even Salem until the evening when the spell wore off.

Sabrina sat up, fluffed her pillow, and then sank back into it again. Try as she might, she just could not get comfortable.

Instead of being happy that Salem was out of her

hair for the night, Sabrina felt guilty. Here she was, warm and comfortable in a cozy bed while Salem was out in the cold. What would her aunts say about what she'd done? They complained about Salem a lot, but Sabrina couldn't remember a time when they wouldn't let him in the house.

At 2:30, Sabrina decided to un-cast the spell and let Salem back into the house. At 2:31 she remembered that casting and un-casting spells so quickly could be dangerous, and she changed her mind. Sabrina vowed to let Salem in first thing the next morning. She'd even point up one of his favorite breakfasts: beef Wellington, or baked Alaska, or a tuna fish BLT. Salem had so many favorite dishes, it was hard to keep track of them all. But no matter, Sabrina would just ask him.

Now that her conscience was clear, Sabrina felt her eyelids grow heavy. It was a struggle to keep them open, so she stopped trying. And soon sleep overtook her.

"Hey, sleepyhead?"

Sabrina opened her eyes. Bright light streamed in through the windows, and a dark-haired figure was standing at the foot of her bed. Sabrina blinked and rubbed her eyes. It was Roxie, dressed in green army pants and a long-sleeved black shirt.

"What time is it?" Sabrina mumbled.

"It's ten o'clock. I wouldn't have woken you, but last night you'd said you wanted to hit the books pretty early."

Sabrina propped herself up on her elbows. "No, you're right. Thanks for getting me up."

"Are you working on history all day?" asked Roxie.

"The plan is to avoid all contact with humans," said Sabrina.

Roxie flashed Sabrina a suspicious glance. "What did you say?"

"I mean, yes, I'm going to study all day," said Sabrina. "After I let Salem back into the house and apologize."

"Apologize to your cat?" asked Roxie. "I guess you have been kind of harsh to him lately. Poor guy."

Sabrina covered her mouth and buried her head under her pillow. "Too early. Can't speak," she mumbled.

"Whatever," said Roxie, leaving the room. "I'm off to tape *Chick Chat*. Catch you later."

Sabrina changed into a pair of black cords and a

purple sweater and then walked outside. "Salem," she called. "Are you ready for breakfast?"

She'd expected Salem to come running, but strangely he didn't even answer her.

Walking back into the house she found Morgan in the kitchen polishing off a cranberry orange muffin. "Have you seen Salem?" she asked.

"Not lately," said Morgan. "What happened to you last night? How come you bailed so early? The party was just getting started."

Sabrina had to answer. "It was kind of loud for my tastes. I guess I just wasn't in the mood to have mindless conversations with frat boys."

"But you did end up leaving with a certain frat boy, right?" said Morgan, her eyebrows raised.

Sabrina shook her head. "Trust me, it's not what you think. That was Jason—a guy from my poetry workshop. We're friends."

"Are you telling me you're not attracted to him at all?" asked Morgan.

Sabrina decided to employ her diversion technique. "So," she said, "what happened with your sociology TA? You guys were looking pretty tight on the dance floor."

Morgan rolled her eyes. "Yeah, that is so over."

"How come?" asked Sabrina, sincerely interested and glad that the direction of the conversation had changed.

"He gave me a ride home after the party," said Morgan. "And his car—it was so lame. A Hyundai."

"You're not going to go out with him because you didn't like his car? That's so shallow!" Sabrina immediately covered her mouth and cringed. She hadn't wanted to speak the truth—at least not so blatantly.

Lucky for her, though, Morgan seemed okay with the accusation. Shrugging, she asked, "And what's your point? Why don't you tell me something I don't know?"

Sabrina walked outside to continue her search for Salem. "Don't be mad at me," she called once the door was closed. "I'm really sorry." Pointing, Sabrina conjured up a pair of binoculars and peered through the lenses. No sign of the cat.

Sabrina had the sneaking suspicion that Salem's absence wasn't accidental, that he was missing and it was all her fault.

Just then, Morgan opened up the front door. "Phone for you," she said, handing Sabrina the cordless. "Hey, where did you get those binoculars?"

Ignoring the question, Sabrina took the phone and sat down on the porch swing. "Hello?"

"It's Zelda calling," her aunt said.

"Aunt Zelda! It's such a surprise to hear from you," said Sabrina. "How is the cruise?"

"Honestly?" asked Zelda.

Sabrina suppressed her laughter. "Yes, honestly. It's the theme of the week."

"What do you mean?" asked Zelda.

Sabrina clamped her hand over her mouth before she spilled the beans. Luckily, Zelda didn't pursue the issue.

"Anyway, dear. I'll make this quick because my phone card is running out—you wouldn't believe the Other Realm-to-Mortal Realm rates these days! In short—we'll be home around eight o'clock."

"You are?" asked Sabrina. "That's horrible!"

"Why is it horrible?" asked Zelda.

"Um . . ." Sabrina stalled, trying to come up with a new truth. "Because you two hardly ever take vacations. So it's kind of a bummer that you feel the need to cut this one short."

"Thank you for your concern," said Zelda. "But the cruise really isn't what we thought it would be. Plus, I feel bad leaving Patricia to do all of that work alone. She's bailed me out a number of times, and I should really be helping her."

"Okay," said Sabrina weakly. "You have a point there. I guess you'd want me to keep Salem, though. I mean, since he and Patricia can't see each other."

"Actually," said Zelda, "I thought we'd bring him home. I know he can be a handful. It's not fair for you to have to deal with him when you have so much else going on in your life. We'll just zap up a temporary wing for the lab under the basement. That way we can keep Patricia and Salem apart."

"Really," said Sabrina, attempting to cover her mouth, "that would be great, as long as you could find him."

"What do you mean?" asked Zelda.

Sabrina clamped her hand over her mouth.

"Hello?" said Zelda. "We must have a bad connection."

"No, it's fine," said Sabrina. "It will be good to see you. Bring me one of those novelty rings from Saturn, will you?"

Sabrina hung up the phone.

"You were talking to someone on Saturn?" asked Miles, who on his way out the front door couldn't help but overhear the end of Sabrina's conversation.

Sabrina panicked, wondering why, of all her housemates, it had to be Miles who had heard her talking to her aunts. "Saturns are very safe cars, you know."

"What does that have to do with anything?" asked Miles.

"It's too bad you have that zit on your chin," said Sabrina, immediately regretting her words. She didn't mean to insult Miles, but she was under pressure and had to say the first thing that came to her mind.

Miles covered up his chin with one hand. "You know, I used to think you were the nice one around here."

"It's really not that noticeable," said Sabrina.

"Really?" asked Miles.

"Yeah, especially next to the one on your nose."

"I've got to call my dermatologist," said Miles, running back into the house and slamming the door behind him.

Sabrina sighed. She felt truly awful. Insulting Miles was the last thing she wanted to do. Even though her comments were insensitive, she was glad she was able to distract him from the bigger truth.

But Sabrina had bigger problems to worry about.

She had to find Salem before her aunts got home. Otherwise, the consequences would be dire. They'd find out that she'd not only lost Salem, but also that she'd mis-cast another spell.

For a brief moment she considered going back into her house, to search the WWW for a good spell to trace Salem. Remembering what had happened the last time she'd used magic, though, Sabrina thought better of it.

Instead, she headed toward campus. She didn't know if she'd find Salem there, but it seemed like a good place to start. Plus, she'd get to avoid her housemates for a while. She'd insulted them all enough, and didn't want to stick around and risk doing any more damage. Not when she had ten more hours until the Honesty Spell wore off.

☆

Chapter 9

☆

Sabrina searched Salem's favorite Dumpsters—the ones behind the school cafeteria—but she found no trace of him. She tried the library, where he sometimes liked to shoot spitballs at students trying to study, but he wasn't there, either. On her way to the athletic fields, where Salem liked to watch the women's field hockey team practice, she ran into Harvey.

"What are you doing here?" she asked with surprise.

"I go to school nearby—Emerson College, remember? It's just a mile from here."

"I know," said Sabrina, not in the mood to fool around.

Harvey's familiar sweet smile faded, and his face flashed concern. "What's going on?"

Sabrina took a deep breath. Harvey was the one mortal—besides Sabrina's mother—who knew she was a witch. Maybe he could help.

"I'm under an honesty spell and Salem is missing and my aunts are coming home from Saturn in an hour, so I only have that long to find him," said Sabrina. She breathed a sigh of relief, happy that for once she could be honest without a penalty.

Harvey just laughed.

"What?" Sabrina snapped.

He shook his head. "Whenever I ask you what's going on, it's never just, 'Oh, not much.'"

"This is serious, Harvey," said Sabrina. "Will you help me find him?"

"Sure," said Harvey, trying to wipe the smile off his face. Crossing his arms over his chest, he asked, "Where did you see him last?"

"Salem was on the front porch when I walked home with Jason last night and—" Sabrina clamped her hand over her mouth.

"Who's Jason?" asked Harvey.

"He's a guy in my poetry workshop," said Sabrina, wanting to change the subject, fast.

"You're in a poetry workshop?"

"I was," said Sabrina. "Now I'm not so sure.

Actually, it's the workshop that got me into this whole mess. Well, sort of."

"What happened?" asked Harvey.

"Can we find Salem first and talk later?" asked Sabrina.

"You're the boss," said Harvey with a shrug.

"Right," said Sabrina, pacing back and forth. "I checked Salem's usual spots, and there's just no trace of him. He can't be at my house, because I put a spell on him, banning him from entering."

"You did what?" said Harvey, clearly taken aback.

"He deserved it. Trust me," said Sabrina. "I've been taking care of him since yesterday, and he's been totally impossible."

"Maybe he went to your aunts' house," said Harvey.

"I hope not," said Sabrina with a groan. "His ex-fiancée is there, and if she sees him, she'll flip."

Harvey raised his eyebrows and shook his head—amazed that Sabrina's life was so complicated.

"We might as well check, though," said Sabrina. "I don't know where else to go."

She looked over her shoulder. Since no one was looking, she pointed herself and Harvey to her aunts' doorstep.

"I've seen you do this kind of thing a hundred times, but I can't help but be amazed," Harvey said as he looked at her aunts' house.

"Remember, don't say anything about Salem," said Sabrina. "I don't want to upset Patricia."

Sabrina put her key in the door but, before opening it, said, "I'll distract her, and you search for Salem, okay?"

Harvey nodded. "Wait!" he said. "Before you open the door, tell me, is Patricia one of those freaky-looking Other Realm people? Because I want to be prepared."

"No," said Sabrina. "Well, on her own planet Ingraft—she takes the form of something that looks like liquid mercury. But here, she morphs into a mortal body."

"Cool," said Harvey, nodding his head.

"Whatever you do, don't mention Salem," said Sabrina.

"Sure," said Harvey.

She pushed the door open to find Patricia in Zelda's lab pouring the contents of one beaker into another beaker. "Patricia!" Sabrina said. "Long time no see."

Patricia raised her goggles to her forehead, peeled

off her gloves, and smiled. Sabrina hadn't mentioned that Patricia's Mortal Realm form was that of a supermodel. But Harvey didn't protest. In fact, he was speechless.

Shaking out her beautiful blond curls, Patricia rushed forward and, since she was six feet tall, bent down to give Sabrina a hug. "It's so wonderful to see you!"

"Good to see you, too, Patricia," Sabrina said. "This is my friend Harvey Kinkle."

"Hello, Harvey," said Patricia, shaking Harvey's hand.

"Hi." His voice came out as a croak.

"How's the work coming?" asked Sabrina.

Patricia sighed and shook her head. Her large green eyes looked sad. "Good, but not great. I've made a lot of progress this weekend, but I can't find the right ingredient for this formula I'm working on."

"That's too bad," said Sabrina.

"Well, I still have another week to find it before my deadline."

"At least you're not under any pressure," Harvey joked.

Patricia turned to him and frowned. "Actually, I'm under a lot of pressure."

Sabrina whispered to Harvey, "There's no such thing as sarcasm on Planet Ingraft."

"Now you tell me," said Harvey.

"So what brings you both to Hilda and Zelda's?" asked Patricia.

Sabrina's eyes widened in horror when she realized she was still under the Honesty Spell and couldn't let slip that she was searching for Salem. That would surely jeopardize Patricia's research. Covering her mouth with her hands, she glared at Harvey.

"Um," said Harvey, "I left my basketball here last week."

"Really," said Patricia. "How odd."

"Yes," said Harvey, shrugging at Sabrina. "Sabrina, why don't you look upstairs for it, and I'll check around down here."

"Good idea, Harvey," said Sabrina. "I'm glad I ran into you. Don't mind us, Patricia."

Twenty minutes later, Sabrina and Harvey had combed every inch of the Spellman home and Salem was still nowhere to be found.

"Any luck?" Sabrina asked, jogging down the steps.

"I can't find him anywhere," Harvey said with a sigh.

"Him?" asked Patricia.

"I call my basketball Rover," Harvey said quickly.

"How odd," said Patricia, turning back to her work.

Sabrina grabbed Harvey's arm and pulled him toward the door. "Great to see you, Patricia. Good luck with everything. I'm keeping my fingers crossed."

"Bye-bye, dear. I hope you find whatever you're looking for," Patricia called.

"That was a close one," Sabrina said once they were outside again.

"No kidding," said Harvey.

"A basketball named Rover?" asked Sabrina.

"Hey, I was on the spot," said Harvey.

Sabrina glanced at her watch. "My aunts will be back tonight and still no Salem."

"Let's check around Adams College again. You never know," said Harvey.

As they made their way across the football field, a Frisbee landed at Sabrina's feet. Jason ran up to her. Hatless today, his blond hair flopped with each step.

"Hey Jason," she said.

"Hi," said Jason, giving Harvey a glance.

"This is my friend Harvey," said Sabrina.

"Nice to meet you, Harvey," said Jason. Turning back to Sabrina he added, "Thanks for changing your mind last night, by the way."

"Huh?" asked Sabrina.

"Thanks for lending Salem to the house. We'll take good care of him. You have nothing to worry about," said Jason.

"I didn't change my mind," said Sabrina.

"Really?" said Jason, a little taken aback. "Because he was standing on the back porch, so I just assumed you left him there."

Sabrina shook her head. "Salem must have wandered over to the party by himself."

"You're kidding!" asked Jason. "What are the odds?"

"Was there any food on the back porch?" asked Sabrina.

Jason shrugged. "I think there may have been some pizza outside."

Sabrina shook her head. "We'd better go get him. My aunts are coming home any minute and they really want to take Salem off my hands."

"Oh, that's so sweet," said Jason. "Are they coming home early because they miss him?"

Sabrina wanted to say yes, but of course that

would be a lie. Luckily, though, Harvey picked up the conversation where she couldn't. "That's exactly it," he said as Sabrina covered her mouth with both hands. "Zelda and Hilda are crazy about Salem. They can hardly tear themselves away from him."

"Or turn their backs on him," Sabrina couldn't help but add.

Jason looked from Harvey to Sabrina. "Well, if you guys follow me, I'll show you to the house. He's in my room because it turns out one of the guys in the fraternity house is allergic to cats."

As soon as they made their way into the house, Sabrina couldn't help but scrunch up her face and blurt out, "It really stinks in here." Harvey elbowed her gently, and she replied with a shrug.

"I know," said Jason. "It takes a couple of days for the house to air out after parties."

They made their way upstairs, and Jason opened up a door at the end of the hall. "Salem?" he called. "Here, kitty, kitty . . ."

"Salem doesn't respond to 'kitty,'" said Sabrina.

"Apparently Salem doesn't respond to anything," said Harvey, glancing around the room.

"He's not here," said Jason, looking almost as distressed as Sabrina.

"My aunts are going to flip!"

"Hey, Sid?" Jason ran down the stairs, and Harvey and Sabrina followed him. They ended up in a wood-paneled room with two beat-up old couches by the window and a pool table in its center. On top of the pool table was a large, sleeping frat boy.

"Wake up, Sid," said Jason.

"Huh?" Sid, a tall guy with reddish curls, sat up.

"What happened to that cat I brought home yesterday?" asked Jason.

"Cat?" said Sid.

"Small cute little black thing," said Jason. "Walks on four legs. Has a long skinny tail."

"Oh yeah," said Sid, scratching his head. "I saw it this morning."

"Where did you see him?" asked Sabrina, running out of patience.

"Jon Bank took her," said Sid.

"Him," said Sabrina. "It's a him."

Harvey put a hand on Sabrina's shoulder, hoping to calm her down. "It's cool," he said in a whisper. "We'll find him."

"We have to," Sabrina hissed back.

"I'm so sorry about this," said Jason.

"Who is Jon Bank?" asked Sabrina, shaking Sid.

"And what did he do with Salem?"

"It's cool. Relax," said Sid, backing away from Sabrina. "Jon took him to the Alpha Delta Sigma house."

"Huh?" asked Sabrina and Harvey at the same time.

"It's an Emerson sorority," Sid explained. "Jon totally forgot it was his girlfriend's birthday. He saw the cat and decided it would be a perfect gift."

"Really perfect," said Sabrina.

"It's okay," said Jason. "Their house is just a few blocks away. I can show you."

"We can find it. I'm sure Harvey knows where it is," said Sabrina.

"I'm so sorry about this," said Jason. "I feel horrible."

"You didn't mean it," said Sabrina. "I know it was an accident."

"Will I see you in Max's workshop next week?" asked Jason.

"I don't know," Sabrina said, in all honesty, as she made her way out the door.

Chapter 10

Sabrina knocked on the door of the Alpha Delta Sigma house and was greeted by a familiar face. Amber, from her poetry workshop, was standing in front of her—dressed like she was staying in to study all day. Her dark hair was swept up in a high ponytail, and she was wearing navy blue sweatpants and a gray T-shirt. "Sabrina, what are you doing here?" Amber's whole face lit up when she smiled.

"I didn't know you lived here," said Sabrina.

"I moved in last semester. How are you doing?"

"To be honest," Sabrina said, walking into the house past Amber and looking around, "I'm sort of stressed. You wouldn't believe the weekend I'm having."

Amber looked at Sabrina curiously, wondering why she was being so candid. "Is there something I can do to help?"

"I hope so. You see, there's been this big misunderstanding, and I sort of lost my cat. This is Harvey, by the way."

Harvey blushed as he waved a hello from the doorstep.

"Come on in," said Amber.

"Who's at the door?" asked another sorority girl as she made her way down the stairs. She was pretty, dark, and athletic, with long wavy black hair and intense brown eyes.

"Maria, this is my friend Sabrina, and this is Harvey," said Amber. "They're looking for their cat."

"He's all black," said Sabrina. "He has these yellow eyes, and he really likes scrunchies. He just disappeared last night, and I was told he might be here."

"Nothing like that here," said Maria, shaking her head.

Amber's green eyes flashed concern as she looked back and forth between them. "Where is that cat that Jon gave you?" she asked Maria gently.

"You mean Fluffy?" Maria said, crossing her arms over her chest. "Last I checked, he was eating his second breakfast. He sure has an appetite. But Fluffy was a stray cat. He can't be yours."

"Fluffy?" asked Sabrina.

Just then, Salem scampered into the room. Sabrina was surprised that he was wearing a bright blue bow around his neck with a matching cap. "Salem!" she said.

Salem hissed at her and leaped into Maria's arms.

Sabrina rolled her eyes, frustrated that she had finally found Salem and he wasn't going to make things easy for her.

Amber looked from Maria to Sabrina. "Are you sure that's your cat?" she asked. "Because he doesn't seem to like you very much."

"We're sure," said Harvey.

Maria held Salem protectively, and he curled up in her arms. "I was just knitting him a sweater upstairs."

Sabrina pointed and froze everyone in the room but herself and Salem. "What are you doing?" she asked him.

"Just trying to spend some time with those who really want me around," Salem said.

Sabrina crossed her arms over her chest. "Salem, I'm so sorry I locked you out of the house last night."

"'Sorry' isn't going to cut it," said Salem.

"What do you want?" asked Sabrina.

"Cold, hard cash," he answered.

"Oh come on, I make a dollar over minimum wage at Hilda's Coffeehouse. You know that."

"That's not including tips," said Salem.

"I really feel horrible about the way I've been treating you. It's this honesty spell. It brings out the worst in me!" Backpedaling, she added, "That's not exactly what I meant to say."

"Oh, but it is," said Salem, looking very comfortable in Maria's arms.

"You want honesty?" asked Sabrina. "How about this? I was awake all night, racked with guilt. This morning I woke up and the first thing I planned to do was apologize and then conjure up the meal of your choice."

Salem looked at the clock. "You're still under the spell, so I can't exactly accuse you of being insincere. So tell me, why are you really here?"

"Hilda and Zelda are on their way home. Their cruise was kind of a bust."

"Well," said Salem, "I have it pretty good here at the sorority house. Why would I want to go back there?"

Sabrina let out a breath in frustration. "Please come home. Don't make me beg."

"Until a minute ago you couldn't wait to get rid of me."

"Well yeah," said Sabrina. "What do you expect when you've been acting so mean—taunting Miles, eating my housemates' food, getting me in trouble with everyone."

"You're the one who messed up the Honesty Spell," said Salem.

"Which has made things twice as stressful. Look, if you don't come with me now, I'm going to have to tell my aunts what happened, and I really don't want to do that," Sabrina said, despite herself. She realized this was not the best argument to get Salem home.

"So you're just as self-interested as I am," said Salem.

"That's not the whole story," said Sabrina.

"I don't know," said Salem in a voice that told Sabrina he really enjoyed the position she was in.

"I've really felt guilty about how I've been treating you," said Sabrina, suddenly noticing something strange. "Hey, what's that on your nails? Are they purple?"

Salem hid his paws under his chin. "Nobody's perfect, you know."

"You're letting sorority girls paint your nails?" asked Sabrina. "Where is your self-respect?"

"I like the attention," Salem sniffed. "Plus, this polish has extra nutrients to harden nails."

"Fine, have it your way." Sabrina pointed and unfroze time.

The mortals continued their conversation where they had left off.

"Sabrina, I wonder why he isn't going to you when you call," Amber said curiously.

"I think he's mad at me," said Sabrina. "We had a little argument last night, and he's a very vengeful cat."

"That's a horrible thing to say about a poor little kitty," said Maria in a baby voice that made Sabrina cringe.

"He's not your typical cat," said Sabrina, glaring at Harvey, hoping he'd cut in.

"Some people think he's cursed," said Harvey.

Maria and Amber looked at him like he was crazy.

"Seriously," said Harvey. "It happens. Curses, I mean. This guy on my hockey team went to Hawaii and found this strange necklace. He put it on, and then crazy things started happening."

"Like what?" asked Amber.

"His brother was bitten by a tarantula, and then he got into a surfing accident and hit his head."

"That sounds strangely familiar," said Maria. "Was his name Greg?"

"Yes," said Harvey, nodding his head frantically. "Do you know him?"

"No, but I saw that episode of *The Brady Bunch* on Nick at Nite," said Maria, rolling her eyes.

"Have you noticed anything strange since Salem moved in here?" asked Sabrina, wanting to change the subject, fast.

"You mean Fluffy," Maria corrected her.

Sabrina shrugged. "Sure, Fluffy. Call him whatever you want."

Amber bit her bottom lip and glanced at Maria nervously. "Tell them," she whispered.

Maria shook her head.

"Please," said Harvey. "We've been honest with you."

"Okay," said Maria, setting Salem down on the couch. "Things *have* been a little weird since the kitty moved in."

"It's not that we're superstitious," said Amber. "It's just that, well, ever since Jon brought him over, I feel like I'm being watched."

"He seems to understand what we're saying," said Maria. "You can almost have a conversation with him."

Sabrina nodded. "I hate to admit it, but he's very intelligent." Pretending to cough, she covered her mouth with her hand before she said anything too revealing.

"Have you noticed that he's got quite an appetite?" Harvey asked.

"It's true," said Maria. "He figured out how to open up the refrigerator, and now it's empty."

"Geh?" said Salem.

Suddenly all eyes were on him.

"That was creepy," said Amber, looking at Salem cautiously.

"Maybe Colleen was right," Amber whispered to Maria.

"Who's Colleen?" asked Sabrina.

"She's a friend of ours. Another sister," Maria explained. "She said she came downstairs early this morning and found Salem on the phone. We told her she was crazy, but I don't know. . . ."

"Look, we're really sorry to bother you," said Harvey. "But I think you should give Salem to us. He's not normal. And I can't see him being very good for the house."

"If he's so bad, why do you want him?" asked Amber.

It was a good question, and Sabrina and Harvey were momentarily stumped. "He's my aunts' cat," said Sabrina, the first to recover. "And they're pretty good at controlling him. Well, better than I am, anyway."

Salem pleaded with his eyes.

When Maria looked at Amber quizzically, Amber sprang to Sabrina's defense. "Look, I know this girl, and she's not crazy. She's in my poetry workshop and she's pretty cool. I'm sure she's being honest with us."

Sighing, Maria handed Salem to Sabrina. "Okay, if you say he's yours, we're not going to argue."

"Thank you," said Sabrina. "You're being very wise. Trust me. It's better that you give him up now. Before the phone bill gets too high." She covered her mouth again.

"I think we should go," said Harvey, backing up.

"Right. Thanks for your help," said Sabrina, making her way out the door.

"I'll see you Thursday," said Amber.

"Thursday?" said Sabrina.

"At the poetry workshop."

"Oh," said Sabrina. "I don't think I'm going to make it."

"Why not?" asked Amber.

Backed into a corner, Sabrina answered truthfully. "I worked to hard on my poem and I felt like no one really got it. I mean, some people weren't even listening when I read it." Sabrina clamped her hand over her mouth when she realized that Amber had been one of those people.

"I've been meaning to apologize about that. I don't know what came over me last week. But I read your poem yesterday," Amber said. "And I thought it was really beautiful."

"Really?" asked Sabrina.

"Really," said Amber. "I think it's topical, too. Living in a city, not many people think about the beauty and endurance of nature all around us."

"You really got it!" Sabrina said with a gasp.

"Of course," said Amber. "It was obvious. Probably because you're such a good writer."

"Do you really think so?" asked Sabrina. "Wait, never mind. You said it, so I'll believe you. Thanks, Amber. And I'll see you Thursday."

"Bye," Amber said as she closed the door.

"What was that all about?" asked Harvey as they headed back to Sabrina's aunts' house.

"It's a long story," said Sabrina. "To be honest, I'd rather not talk about it."

Once they made it to the Spellman home, Harvey said good-bye.

"Aren't you coming in?" asked Sabrina.

Harvey shook his head. "I've had enough weirdness for today. Plus, I have a history paper to write. Unless you want to point one up for me," he asked hopefully.

Sabrina shook her head. "I think I've used enough magic for a while."

Harvey shrugged. "Suit yourself."

"Okay," said Sabrina. "Thanks for all your help."

"See you around," said Harvey.

Sabrina took a deep breath and stared up at the house.

"What are you waiting for?" asked Salem.

"I'm trying to figure out how to get you inside without Patricia seeing you," said Sabrina.

"You could have just left me at the sorority house," Salem sniffed. "They were going to rent *Blue Crush* and make Rice Krispies Treats tonight."

☆

Chapter 11

☆

"Sabrina!" Hilda exclaimed as she opened the front door and then rushed outside. She was still in her cruise gear: a floppy straw hat and a yellow sundress. She was also bright red and emanating a faint glow.

Sabrina gave her aunt a hug. "Aunt Hilda. Welcome back! What happened to you?"

"I got a little too close to the sun," said Hilda. "You should see Zelda, though. She's burned worse than I am."

"Ah-hem!" said Salem from where he stood next to Sabrina.

"Yes?" Hilda said.

"I don't get a hello?"

"Oh hello," said Hilda dryly.

"Nice to know I'm loved," said Salem.

"Is it safe to go inside?" asked Sabrina, peering into the house.

Hilda pointed and conjured up two pairs of sunglasses—one Salem sized and one Sabrina sized. "You guys should put these on first. Zelda is brighter than a one-thousand-watt lightbulb."

Taking the glasses, Sabrina whispered, "I meant because of the Patricia-Salem issue."

"Not to worry," said Hilda. "Patricia and Zelda are hard at work in a new subterranean lab below the basement. She's got no idea that we live with her ex. And she's got no intention of leaving the lab until she finishes with her work."

"Phew," said Sabrina. Salem scampered into the living room, heading straight for the computer.

"What are you doing?" asked Hilda.

"Some online dating," said Salem. "Things didn't work out with my last love."

Hilda rolled her eyes, but Sabrina was too happy to get bent out of shape. She had survived her weekend with Salem and, even better, she was off the hook.

"So how was he?" asked Hilda. "I can imagine he must have been a handful."

"Salem was a perfect angel!" Sabrina couldn't

believe what had just come out of her mouth! She looked at her watch and realized it was 8:30 and that the truth spell had worn off.

"Really?" said Hilda.

Sabrina nodded, saying, "Absolutely."

"We did it!" yelled Zelda. As she came into the room, it brightened up as if she had turned on a dozen halogen lamps.

Sabrina slipped on her sunglasses. "That was fast," she said.

"Sabrina! It's so good to see you," Zelda said. "I'd hug you, but then I'd burn you."

"So have you finished up in the lab?" asked Sabrina.

"We have," said Patricia, entering the room. Turning to Sabrina she asked, "Did you and Harvey ever find Rover?"

"Yes," said Sabrina.

"Who's Rover?" asked Hilda.

"Long story. I'll explain later," said Sabrina, thrilled that she didn't blurt out the truth.

"Can you guys keep it down? I'm on the Net looking for love," quipped Salem.

Zelda looked at Salem, wide-eyed. She quickly pointed and made him invisible.

"Who was that?" Patricia asked suspiciously. "I've heard that voice before."

"No one," said Sabrina. "Tell me about your experiment. What finally worked?"

Patricia shook her head. "You're all hiding something. What is it?"

"It's nothing," said Zelda, placing a hand on Patricia's shoulder. "We should get back downstairs."

Patricia shook her head. "I'm not going anywhere until someone explains."

Zelda sighed. Pointing, she made Salem visible.

"You were hiding a cat? I've seen cats before. It's not my first time to the Mortal Realm, you know."

Salem sighed and hung his head. "It's me, Salem. They were trying to protect you."

Sabrina and her aunts braced themselves for the inevitable hysteria.

As expected, Patricia turned bright red. She took a deep breath and clasped her hands behind her neck. Sabrina and her aunts were afraid she was going to break down and cry.

But she surprised them.

Patricia began to laugh hysterically. Tears streamed down her face, but they were ones of joy.

"I was heartbroken and depressed over you. I wasted years mourning over the future we never had. And here you are—a common house cat. I wish I had known that before."

"Watch who you're calling 'common,'" Salem said. "I'm loved by sorority sisters all over this town."

Patricia couldn't control her laughter.

Salem was so annoyed, he went upstairs to hide.

"Poor guy," said Hilda. "And after he acted like such an angel while we were away."

Suddenly, something dawned on Sabrina. She decided to be honest with her aunts. "Actually," she said, "Salem was a nightmare."

"Really?" said Zelda.

Sabrina smiled. She was no longer under the Honesty Spell, but she decided to tell her aunts everything. Not just about Salem, either. She told them about her poetry workshop, about the Honesty Spell and the repercussions, about unintentionally insulting all of her housemates, and even about losing Salem to a fraternity house.

"Sounds like you've had quite an adventure," said Hilda, zapping up four banana splits. Hers and Zelda's had an extra scoop of ice cream each, to help them cool off. Patricia's had extra whipped cream since she had finished her work so early. And Sabrina's had extra caramel sauce since she'd proven herself to be so good at handling an extra-sticky situation.

"And it sounds like you learned a very important lesson," said Zelda, digging into her sundae.

Sabrina nodded. "It's so true. Honesty isn't always the best policy. I mean, life is much more complicated than that. Sometimes stretching the truth is necessary to, you know, avoid insulting people."

"And sometimes using magic to make life better just leads to further complications and more problems," Zelda added.

"Ah-hem!" Patricia cleared her throat.

"What?" asked Sabrina.

"I think we all learned a lesson," said Patricia, glancing toward Zelda and Hilda. "I know you were trying to protect me, but I wish you'd been more honest from the beginning."

Zelda hung her head. "You are so right."

Patricia continued. "The truth is, I got over Salem years ago. I learned to move on with my life, and even if he was still his old handsome self, I would have been able to handle it."

Just then, Salem scampered into the room. "No dessert for me?" he asked.

Sabrina pointed him a bowl of dried cat food.

"Surely you're joking," he said.

"I don't know." Zelda asked Patricia, "What do you think?"

"I hold no grudges," said Patricia. "Salem can have his ice cream." Grinning mischievously, Patricia pointed up a sundae for Salem.

He dug in greedily, but raised his head a few moments later. "Something's wrong here," he said. "What kind of ice cream is this?"

"Dry cat food–flavored," said Patricia. "I hold no grudges, but I'm also a big believer in 'just desserts.'"

"Geh?" said Salem.